EARLY MAN

THE JUNIOR NOVELIZATION

Sky Pony Press
New York

First published in the U.K. by Igloo Books, 2018.

This paperback edition published by Sky Pony Press, 2018.

Sky Pony Press books may be purchased in bulk at special discounts for sales promotion, corporate gifts, fund-raising, or educational purposes. Special editions can also be created to specifications. For details, contact the Special Sales Department, Sky Pony Press, 307 West 36th Street, 11th Floor, New York, NY 10018 or info@skyhorsepublishing.com.

Sky Pony® is a registered trademark of Skyhorse Publishing, Inc.®, a Delaware corporation.

Visit our website at www.skyponypress.com

10 9 8 7 6 5 4 3 2 1

Library of Congress Cataloging-in-Publication Data available on file.

Text by Richard Dungworth
Jacket and interior illustration by Aardman Animation
Jacket, interior, and insert design by Matt Hamilton

Paperback ISBN: 978-1-5107-3538-5
E-book ISBN: 978-1-5107-3540-8

Printed in Canada

CONTENTS

Prologue: Earth. The Prehistoric Age 5

Chapter One: Meet the Tribe 9

Chapter Two: Lord Nooth Muscles In 21

Chapter Three: The City of Bronze 29

Chapter Four: The Sacred Game 37

Chapter Five: A Late Challenge 47

Chapter Six: Tribe In Training 57

Chapter Seven: Goona Hits the Spot 69

Chapter Eight: Pig Trouble 77

Chapter Nine: Ball Skills, Badlands Style! 83

Chapter Ten: The Awful Truth.............................. 93

Chapter Eleven: Dug's Choice 101

Chapter Twelve: Game On!................................. 109

Chapter Thirteen: Brilliant Bronzio 115

Chapter Fourteen: The Tribe, United 123

Chapter Fifteen: Champions! 133

Epilogue: Overtime 141

PROLOGUE

EARTH. THE PREHISTORIC AGE . . .

In the vast blackness of space, a small blue-green world slowly circles its burning sun.

It is a harsh, restless world. Fiery volcanoes cloud its sky with ash. Earthquakes shake and split its surface. Its one great continent, surrounded by a single ocean, is slowly tearing apart.

Dinosaurs rule this volcanic, steam-misted land. But other creatures, too, survive among the lava flows and hot springs. Here, look, is a group of ape-like brutes, Neanderthals, fighting over their latest kill.

Something is about to rock their world.

In space, a meteor is hurtling toward them.

The unsuspecting Neanderthals go on bashing, gobbling, and grunting. Bashing, gobbling, and grunting are what they do best. Evolution still has some way to go before Homo sapiens, the human species, will walk the Earth. Neanderthal life lacks even the basic foundations of human civilization.

But that is about to change.

The speeding meteor reaches Earth's atmosphere. It plummets through it, blazing as it falls. Below, a Neanderthal raises his hairy face to watch the falling space rock draw a fiery arc across the sky. He lets out a puzzled grunt, and a rival steals his hunk of meat while he isn't looking.

KERBOOOOOOOOOOOM!

The meteor hits. Its impact creates a devastating explosion. It takes a long time for the huge dust cloud to settle.

The bravest and most inquisitive of the Neanderthals come to investigate the site of the awesome blast. They climb down the sloping sides of the huge crater it has left. At the very center of the crater lies a small, perfectly round rock, still smoldering. It is all that remains of the meteor.

One brute tries to pick it up and drops it with a grunt of pain. It is far too hot to handle. The hurt Neanderthal kicks the space rock angrily . . .

. . . it rolls toward another Neanderthal . . .

. . . who kicks it to a third . . .

. . . who boots it hard across the crater . . .

. . . sending the whole hairy mob chasing after it, howling with delight at the entertaining new activity they have invented. It is even more fun than bashing.

The joy of it does not fade. As the days steadily pass, the Neanderthals spend many happy hours kicking their meteorite-ball around their crater-field. Rules of play slowly develop. They pick teams. They make goalposts, first from their animal-skin shirts, then from great rocks stood on end.

The crater has become a stadium. Others come to watch. Some try to capture the drama and excitement in primitive art. They paint the highlights of the action on standing stones and on the walls of their caves.

The first step toward human civilization has been taken.

The Beautiful Game has been born.

A FEW AGES LATER . . .

CHAPTER ONE

MEET THE TRIBE

It was the dawn of a beautiful new day in the Valley. *Just the sort of day*, thought Dug, *for a first try at mammoth hunting.*

Dug didn't look like a match for a mammoth. The young, scrawny caveman, with his wild mop of dark brown hair, was the smallest of the Tribe. But Dug had never been afraid to think big.

"Come on, Hognob!" he called to his faithful pet hog. "Let's go wake Bobnar!"

As usual, Dug and Hognob had woken up with the sun. The rest of the Tribe had rather less get-up-and-go. They were all still fast asleep. In his cave,

Bobnar, their kindly old leader, was snoring happily in his hammock—but not for long.

"Chief!" cried Dug, bursting in. "Are you awake, Chief?"

Bobnar tumbled out of his hammock, startled. Hognob jumped on him affectionately. Bobnar was a patient old soul, and used to such rude awakenings. He gave a long-suffering sigh.

"Bit early, isn't it Dug?" he said, rubbing his bleary eyes.

"But Chief . . . we're early man!" beamed Dug.

Dug left Bobnar to pull on his rabbit-skin undies, and went back outside to wake the others. They were huddled in a snoozing heap in the forest clearing that formed the heart of the Tribe's Stone Age settlement.

"Come on, everyone!" called Dug, cheerily emptying a bucketful of cold water over his friends. "Time to get up!"

As Bobnar emerged, blinking, into the daylight, Dug hurried to rejoin him. He put forward his bold suggestion for the morning's hunt.

"A mammoth?" said Bobnar, raising his bushy white eyebrows. "You want us to hunt a five-ton, bone-crushing mammoth?"

Despite hunting for food daily, the Tribe was not very good at it. On a lucky day, they might catch a rabbit, at best. So, to go after a mammoth . . .

"Why not?" said Dug. "We could do it, Chief!"

Bobnar looked unconvinced.

"Look, Dug," he said, drawing Dug's attention to one of the several mighty rocks in the clearing that stood up straight. The standing stones were covered in faded, mossed-over paintings. According to Bobnar, these were the work of the Tribe's distant ancestors, who had lived in the great, bowl-shaped valley long ago, before the growth of the lush plant life that now made it such a wonderful home.

Bobnar pointed to one faded painting. "You don't see our ancestors hunting big things," he told Dug. The group of crudely drawn figures in the scene were chasing after a small, unrecognizable . . . something. Bobnar squinted at it. "They hunted . . . little round beasts," he went on uncertainly. "Of some sort."

Dug, too, peered at his ancestors' mystery prey. Small round things, just like what appeared in almost all the ancient paintings.

"What are those?" wondered Dug aloud.

"Rabbits?" suggested Bobnar, shrugging his shoulders. "I suppose they weren't very good at drawing back then."

By now, the rest of the Tribe was more or less awake. After promising Dug that he would bear his mammoth-hunting idea in mind, Bobnar called them together for their regular morning ritual.

"Morning, everyone! Right, gather around. Grab a spear."

The Tribe hurried eagerly to help themselves from the pile of flint-tipped spears. All except Treebor, the gentle giant among them, who took his with obvious reluctance. He looked at its jagged tip unhappily.

"Ooohh!" he moaned. "It's pointy!"

His formidable mother, Magma, gave him an impatient look. Magma wasn't scared of anything or anyone.

"Oh, Treebor!" she scolded him. "Just get over there!"

Barry, who was barely bright enough to tell which end of a spear was which, lugged a large standing stone with him as he made his way to join the assembly. The stone had a friendly smile drawn on it.

"Morning, Barry!" said Dug. "Mr. Rock coming hunting today, is he?"

"Oh, yeah!" replied Barry with a goofy grin. "He wouldn't miss it for the world."

A pretty young cavewoman in a zebra-stripe fur raised her hand, with a pained look, as she took her place.

"Yes, Gravelle?" said Bobnar.

"Chief, when I put my arm up, it hurts!" whined Gravelle.

"Well, don't do it, then," Bobnar advised her patiently. It was a rare day indeed when Gravelle didn't complain of some new injury or ailment.

Bobnar turned his attention to the ginger-haired, fidgety youngster who had joined the circle.

"Morning, Asbo. Changed your underwear today?"

Asbo needed regular reminders about matters of personal hygiene.

"Yeah, Chief!" he replied, hopping from foot to foot. He gestured to the muscular, gruff-looking individual who had just stomped up beside him. "I swapped underwear with Thongo, Chief!"

Thongo gave a grunt of confirmation. A grunt was Thongo's limit.

Bobnar sighed. "That wasn't quite what . . ." he began, then decided it was pointless. "Never mind."

There was a sudden cry of protest from another person in the Tribe.

"Waiyaiymaaanyuscannaaeeeeeetmaaa!"

The angry outburst of gobbledegook came from the lankiest individual in the group. His neighbor was trying to take a bite out of his leg.

"Grubup, stop it!" said Bobnar firmly. "You can't eat that. That's Eemak."

Grubup, whose simple mind was forever fixed on where he could find his next meal, sulkily let go of the outraged Eemak.

Dug was eager to help restore a little order.

"Heads down, everyone!" he said.

The circle of friends bowed their heads and fell silent.

"Thank you, Dug," said Bobnar. He lowered his gaze himself, then began the blessing.

"We give thanks for our Valley, our home, this precious ground, which sustains us and gives us shelter from the Badlands."

There were grunts of agreement from the others. All among them treasured their valley homeland.

"May we live in peace, balance, and harmony with our forest," Bobnar continued. "And all the creatures we share it with."

With a clap of his hands, he signaled that the blessing was over.

"Okay, let's go and kill something!" he cried eagerly.

The morning's outing in the forest followed the usual pattern of the Tribe's hunting expeditions. It was a total shambles.

Bobnar had spent many hours trying to teach the Tribe the essential skills of rabbit-catching, but only Dug showed even the slightest promise. The others had about as much stealth and cunning as a herd of buffalo.

Fortunately, the Valley was brimming with life. It was only a matter of time before they stumbled on a potential catch. It was Bobnar himself who spotted their prey. A rabbit sat in a clearing just ahead. Taking care not to startle it, Bobnar gave the secret signal—a fake bird call—to let his fellow hunters know.

"Cooo-horr!"

From their hiding places in the forest undergrowth, the others stared blankly at their chief.

Bobnar patiently repeated the call, making it as clear as he could.

"Cooo-horr! Cooo-horr!" he cried, nodding his head toward the rabbit.

The Tribe continued to look completely baffled.

Bobnar tried another approach. He made the silent hand signal he had taught them for "rabbit." When it met with nothing but more puzzled looks, he gave up.

"For Pete's sake . . ." muttered Bobnar to himself in frustration. "A RABBIT!" he shouted at the others, pointing.

The bunny in question looked around in alarm as the excited Tribe immediately broke from cover and charged toward it.

The next few minutes were mayhem. Bobnar tried desperately to coach the others. But they each found their own special way to mess up.

"I've got him!" cried Asbo, hurling a coconut at the rabbit. It missed, rebounded off a large, springy spider's web, and knocked Asbo flat.

"Yoww!" howled Barry, hopping around with an arrow in his backside. His attempt to shoot the bunny had also backfired.

"Woah!" wailed Gravelle as Hognob's enthusiastic pursuit of their prey knocked her off her feet.

Eemak and Thongo ran headlong into one another. *Crunch!* The rabbit escaped them both.

"Waaaiiiiiiaaaiiiyyaaageetwallawazzock!" ranted Eemak, incomprehensibly.

Thongo only grunted.

Treebor fared no better. He was nervously trying to surprise the bunny, as instructed by Bobnar. Instead, it crept up behind him, sending him shrieking in terror into the forest. It had no trouble outsmarting Magma, either, easily dodging her wild efforts to whack it with her club. Dug alone came close to grabbing it, only to be pounced on by Grubup, who wasn't fussy about what or who he caught and ate.

In the end, it was down to an unlikely hero to save the day. The unharmed rabbit was casually making its getaway when . . . *Crash!* It ran straight into Mr. Rock, Barry's solid granite friend, and knocked itself out.

Barry high-fived Mr. Rock with delight.

"Nice job, everyone!" beamed Bobnar. "Especially you, Mr. Rock!" He was always ready to praise a rare success, no matter how it came about. "Rabbit Surprise tonight!"

That night, back at the settlement, the high-spirited Tribe celebrated their triumphant hunt with a rowdy party. They bashed and twanged their primitive musical instruments and stomped out their Stone Age dance moves. Bobnar looked on in satisfaction.

"You see, Dug?" he said to his young friend. "We hunt rabbits, and everybody's happy." Bobnar was eager for Dug to abandon his grand mammoth-hunting ideas. It was better to accept their limits as a tribe. "Look at us!" the old chief went on, and they watched the others bump clumsily into one another as they danced. "At the end of the day, we're a rabbit-hunting tribe."

Before Dug could reply, his ears caught a strange, unsettling sound. It was coming from the forest.

Hognob had heard it, too. He began to growl.

"Shush, everyone! Quiet!" ordered Bobnar urgently, reaching for his trusty wooden club.

The Tribe's partying came to a sudden halt. They listened, eyes widening.

They could all hear the noises now. Loud thumps, like heavy footfalls.

Something huge was coming their way through the darkened forest.

CHAPTER TWO

LORD NOOTH MUSCLES IN

The rumblings and thumpings from within the forest suddenly stopped. In the eerie silence that followed, Bobnar crept toward the edge of the clearing, his club held at the ready. He picked up a small rock, and hurled it into the trees in the direction the noises had come from.

There was a loud *Clang!* as the rock struck something. The anxious Tribe exchanged puzzled looks. The sound was entirely unfamiliar to their Stone Age ears.

A spear came flying from the forest. It pierced Bobnar's wooden club and pinned it to a tree trunk. *Thunk!* More spears quickly followed. They were very different from the Tribe's primitive wood-and-flint ones. They had smooth, polished shafts and shiny tips.

"The rabbits are fighting back!" shrieked Barry.

The thumping footfalls resumed, very close now, shaking the ground. Trees near the edge of the clearing began to topple, crashing down from some mighty force.

"I don't think this is rabbits," murmured Bobnar gravely.

Dug was the first to pull himself together.

"ATTACK!" he cried, grabbing a spear and hurling it toward the forest . . .

. . . just as their mystery enemy came crashing into sight.

Awesome war-beasts thundered into the clearing. They were mammoths, but not like any the Tribe had seen before. Their giant shaggy bodies were protected by gleaming armor, made from plates of some hard, shiny material. Dug's flying spear glanced harmlessly off the armor of the leading beast. *Clang!*

These were the trained fighting-mammoths of the mighty Bronze Army. Mounted on their backs and marching beside them were their metal-

armored and metal-weaponed masters. The invaders had brought terrible machines of destruction with them, too. Swinging bronze wrecking balls smashed anything and everything in their path.

To the Tribe, who had no knowledge of metal, the advancing force was utterly alien, and utterly terrifying. There could be no fighting back against an enemy like this.

"RUN!" bellowed Bobnar.

The Tribe took to their heels, dodging bronze spears and wrecking balls as they fled. Their settlement's ancient standing stones were reduced to rubble behind them as the invaders continued their advance.

"Mr. Rock! Noooooo!" wailed Barry as one mighty mammoth toppled his smiling friend, breaking Mr. Rock in half.

Bobnar dragged the devastated Barry away. "To the Badlands, everyone!" he urged.

"What? Leave the Valley?" said Dug, looking dismayed. The thought was heartbreaking. The Valley was their home.

More terrible crashes of metal shattering stone split the air.

"Just GO!" insisted Bobnar.

As the others obeyed their chief, Dug took one last look back, and his heart missed a beat.

"Hognob!" he cried in horror.

His faithful friend had been left behind. Hognob was still defending the settlement. Even now, the brave hog was blocking the path of an advancing mammoth.

Dug was not about to abandon his best pal. The rest of the Tribe, unaware, was already making their getaway. But Dug turned and sprinted back toward the danger.

He was in the nick of time. His diving tackle bowled Hognob out of harm's way not a moment too soon. They tumbled over together and rolled into a ditch. Grateful to be out of sight, Dug peered from their hiding place. He watched in horror as the Bronze Army continued its attack.

Then, on a signal, the destruction stopped.

One of the mammoths was more richly armored and equipped than the rest. From the luxurious carriage on its back, a ramp swung down. A man dressed in purple robes, a burgundy cloak, and gleaming, bronze-trimmed boots descended. The sash around his bulging belly was buckled with a large bronze clasp. It was clear from the man's smug, arrogant air that he was very much the person in charge.

Dug shrank back as the stranger came striding straight toward the spot where he and Hognob were hiding. The man stopped only meters away, stooped to pick up a fragment of rock from the ground, and examined it with a greedy eye. There were glittering flecks within the rock. The sight of them brought an unpleasant smile to the stranger's face.

"Mmmmm . . ." he purred. "Excellent!"

He turned to give his orders to his waiting assistant.

"All right. Secure the valley," he commanded. "Start mining ore!"

The assistant, an older man with a rather magnificent mustache, looked confused.

"Or . . .? Or what, Lord Nooth?" he asked nervously.

His master scowled at him. "The ore, you fool! Start mining the ore!" he barked. "The metal in the ground!"

The assistant cowered under his master's glare. "Oh, the ore! In the ground! Of course!" he groveled. He gestured in the direction in which the Tribe had fled. "What about the primitives, sire?"

By now, Dug realized, his friends should be well on their way out of the Valley. But they were running from one danger to another.

Lord Nooth knew this, too.

"Let them rot in the Badlands," he said with a nasty smirk. "They are the low-achievers of history with their puny flints and drafty caves. The Age of Stone is over, Dino," he told his assistant, sneering. "Long live the Age of Bronze!"

Dug had heard enough. Lord Nooth's cruel mocking of his Tribe and their way of life filled him with fury. He saw red. With no thought for his own safety, he sprang from the ditch and charged at his enemy.

Lord Nooth was already making his way back toward his mammoth. On his signal, his men began their mining work. The first wrecking ball swung into action . . .

. . . and slammed straight into Dug. It knocked him flying out of sight before Nooth, Dino, or anyone else had even noticed his wild charge.

Lord Nooth climbed the ramp into his mammoth-back carriage.

"Okay, let's get moving!" he demanded. "I'm late for my massage!"

Nooth's mammoth and those of his attendants immediately began to make their way back into the forest, returning the way they had come. Only the men and beasts involved in the mining operation remained behind.

And one howling hog.

Hognob had seen what Lord Nooth and his men had failed to notice. Dug was lying on his back, out cold, in a cart pulled by the last of the departing mammoths. He had been knocked into it by the blow from the wrecking ball. And as the cart trundled away, heading for the unknown, there was nothing poor Hognob, driven back by enemy guards, could do to stop it.

CHAPTER THREE

THE CITY OF BRONZE

When Dug came to, he had a very sore head, and not the slightest idea where he was. He was flat on his back, with the sun in his eyes. Whatever he was lying on seemed to be moving. Unfamiliar sounds came from all around.

The mammoth-drawn cart rattled over a drawbridge and through a mighty gateway as Dug, dazed and confused, sat up. His immediate instinct was to flee, and his heart sank as a pair of giant gates swung closed behind the cart, barring his escape. The gates were made of the same shiny stuff as the gleaming armor of the Valley's invaders.

The gates were, in fact, made of bronze, like so much of the great Bronze City to which Lord Nooth's mammoth train had returned. To Dug, whose life with the Tribe had been one of stone, wood, and animal skin, it seemed like the strange shining material was everywhere he looked. All around him were sights that made his Stone Age mind spin—buildings, streets, countless people bustling about in outlandish, complicated clothing.

A sudden lurch in the cart's motion sent Dug tumbling over its side. As the cart trundled on its way, he picked himself up, head still swimming.

He realized, with dismay, how out-of-place he must look. It was plain to see that his animal-fur one-piece was not the fashion here, as it was in the Valley. He stuck out like a sore thumb. He hastily grabbed a piece of cloth that hung nearby and wrapped it around himself like a shawl. Then he staggered off along the street, trying to take in the exotic, mystifying world in which he found himself.

The street was lined with market stalls selling all kinds of goods, the likes of which Dug had never seen. He stared at the nearest stall's impressive range of tools and weapons, all crafted from shining bronze.

"Multi-purpose pen swords!" cried the stall-holder, displaying one for all to admire. "Very handy for opening bottles, too!"

The next stall belonged to a baker, who was proudly demonstrating an up-to-the-minute bronze-bladed bread-cutter.

"Sliced bread? Wow!" gasped his enthusiastic customer. "That's the best thing since . . . well, ever!"

Dug turned to move on, and . . . *Clang!* He collided with something dangling from the neighboring stall. It was a metal pan.

"Hey! Don't touch the bronze!" barked a stern voice. Dug turned to look blankly at a blonde-haired girl, who appeared to be running the stall.

"The what?"

"The bronze!" snapped the girl, giving him a withering look. "Where have you been, the Stone Age?"

Dug was spared having to reply by a sudden blast of blaring horns. As the grand fanfare died down, the sound of chanting rose to fill the air. All around Dug, the city-folk abandoned what they were doing to put on strange horned headgear and other ceremonial costume pieces, all with the same blue-and-bronze color scheme. As one, they began making their way along the street in a single direction. Stall workers, including the sharp-tongued girl, hastily shut up shop to join the moving, chanting crowd. Dug had no choice but to let himself be swept along by the flow of people.

The street turned a corner, and Dug's eyes widened as he saw what it was the city-folk were flocking toward. A huge, spectacular building towered up ahead. Colorful flags flew from its lofty walls. Wherever Dug looked, he saw stunning statues and ornaments of bronze. He thought of the simple stone circle in which the Tribe gathered for their most important rituals. As the crowd carried him on toward the great temple ahead, he decided that this must be their sacred site.

"Fifty schnookels! Fifty schnookels!"

A man with a foghorn voice and an official look stood beside a gateway in the closest wall of the temple. He was holding out a plate piled with small, glittering objects.

"Voluntary contribution!" he bellowed. "Everyone has to pay! Fifty schnookels."

As Dug drew closer, he saw that each person entering the temple first placed a handful of shiny

discs on the plate. He frowned. Coins, like so much in this strange, alien city, were new to him.

"Fifty?" grumbled a man beside him in the shuffling crowd. He dug some shiny discs from a pocket. "It's gone up again!"

"Daylight robbery!" another voice complained from nearby.

Before he knew it, Dug found that he was approaching the temple entrance. The official rattled his collecting plate in Dug's wide-eyed face.

"Fifty schnookels!" he repeated. "Voluntary contribu—Hey!"

Dug had panicked. Without thinking, he had made a run for it. He darted through the entrance ahead before its sentries could stop him.

"Hey!" yelled the surprised official again. "She hasn't voluntarily contributed! Stop her!" Dug's makeshift shawl, long hair, and stooped posture had given the impression he was an old woman.

Dug didn't move like an old woman. Heart pounding, he weaved his way through the crowd as fast as he could. He ducked through a doorway marked STAFF ONLY, and sprinted along an interior corridor of the temple. He could hear the shouting guards coming after him.

"Oi! Stop!"

Dug heard more footsteps and voices up ahead. A side door halfway along the corridor seemed to offer his only hope of escape. He struggled desperately to open it. Catching its handle by sheer luck, he stumbled through the door . . .

. . . and found himself in a white-walled, steam-filled space. A man was standing nearby under what appeared to be his own personal rain-shower. He was singing loudly, and wasn't wearing a stitch of clothing.

It was Dug's good fortune that the guards, hurrying past the changing-room door, didn't catch the sounds of the scuffle within. Shortly, Dug reemerged, looking very different from when he went in. He had stolen the showering man's clothes to disguise himself. In his warrior's cape, badly fitting helmet, and strange studded foot-coverings, he was unrecognizable.

He wasn't out of the woods yet, however. As he ducked into another corridor, several burly men came striding along. They were dressed in capes that matched his own. One was the most handsome man Dug had ever seen. He had long golden hair, an

athletic physique, and a strutting walk that suggested he was well aware just how magnificent he looked.

"I tell you," he was saying to a tough-looking man at his side as they approached Dug, "I wouldn't want to be facing me out there!"

Mr. Magnificent's companion greeted Dug gruffly, mistaking him for the man whose outfit he had on. "Hey, Hugelgraber," he said, rapping his knuckles on Dug's helmet. "Can't you see in that thing? The arena's this way . . ."

Dug had no choice but to turn around and march in the opposite direction. Up ahead, more men stood in a line along one side of the corridor. They, too, had matching headgear and capes, but of a different design than Dug's. Just beyond them, the corridor led out into daylight.

Mr. Magnificent cast a scornful look over the line of men as he, his companions, and Dug formed a second line alongside them.

"You girls are gonna get slaughtered!" he told them with a sneer.

Dug's heart sank. He had a horrible feeling he was about to take part in some sort of violent contest. His present company all had the look of hardened warriors.

Before he could think of a way out, the horn blasts of a mighty fanfare sounded from outside. With a last exchange of fearsome glances, the two lines of men set off at a jog through the opening ahead.

Dug, terrified, was swept helplessly along with them.

CHAPTER FOUR

THE SACRED GAME

The noise and spectacle that greeted Dug as he stumbled back out into daylight took his breath away. The grand fanfare was drowned out by the sudden swell of wild, cheering voices. It was the roar of a mighty crowd.

Dug looked around in bewildered amazement. He was having trouble seeing out through his stolen helmet, but what he could see was enough to make his head spin.

He and the others had emerged in a vast rectangular arena. All around it rose row upon row of tiered seating, jam-packed with noisy citizens.

Dug had never imagined there could be so many people in one place.

The grass surface of the arena itself was unnaturally flat and smooth. For some reason, it had been neatly painted with clean white lines.

Dug struggled to make sense of it all. The vast gathering of this strange and dangerous tribe could only be for some great ritual event. Dug wanted no part in it. He tried to turn back, but the men striding along behind him only bundled him on.

As they paraded out onto the grass, to the very heart of the cauldron of noise, a single voice somehow rose above the din.

"All stand!"

The voice belonged to a man Dug recognized. It was Dino, the finely mustached fellow he had seen assisting Lord Nooth back in the Valley. Dino was standing nearby, speaking into a peculiar contraption. The device magically amplified his voice and projected it around the arena.

"All stand for our mighty leader, Lord Nooth!"

The crowd got to their feet. As their heads turned, Dug followed their gaze. Midway along one long side of the arena was a grand balcony—a private VIP box. A familiar figure, dripping with

bronze bling, stepped out into it. Dug felt a mixture of awe and anger.

Lord Nooth soaked up the crowd's applause as he made his entrance. He moved to the front of the box and raised a hand. A hush fell. Nooth looked down at the two lines of men in the arena below.

"WHO CHALLENGES THE CHAMPIONS?" he bellowed.

The largest of the warriors in the other lineup to Dug's stepped forward. He raised the spear he was holding.

"We challenge the champions!" he roared. He thrust the spear firmly into the ground, at a slant.

Mr. Magnificent immediately responded. He stepped up and planted his own spear, angling it so that its shaft crossed that of his rival's.

"We accept the challenge!" he growled.

It looked more and more likely to the miserable Dug that he was mixed up in some sort of ritual combat. A fight to the death in front of a crowd of strangers was not his idea of fun.

As Dug fretted about just what he'd gotten himself into, and how to get out of it, the crowd turned its attention to a great sundial mounted at one end of the arena. All eyes followed the slowly shifting shadow cast by the sundial's arm.

"The hour has come!" declared Lord Nooth grandly from his box. "Let the Sacred Game commence!"

The dark finger of the sundial's shadow touched the spot marked at the exact center of the grassy arena. A hatch appeared, and a small black-and-white sphere rose into view.

A ball.

Dug stared at it. He didn't have a clue what it was for, and yet something about it seemed vaguely familiar.

He had no time to wonder about this odd feeling of recognition. Things suddenly began to move fast. The men around him threw off their capes. Underneath, they wore matching team uniforms—very short shorts, and numbered tops. They began limbering up, stretching their muscles.

A new announcer's voice echoed around the arena. "Today's match official . . ." it informed the crowd tinnily, ". . . Referee Dino!"

Dino, too, slipped out of his cape, revealing a black shirt and brown shorts. A gleaming bronze whistle hung around his neck. He called the two

men who had performed the spear-crossing ceremony to join him beside the ball. The others jogged off across the grass, spreading out over the arena.

Dug watched, baffled, as Dino flipped a bronze schnookel in the air, caught it again, and peered at it closely.

"In the name of Queen Oofeefa," declared Lord Nooth from his VIP box, "we give thanks for the Beautiful Game!" Nooth was now wearing a bizarre pair of giant fake hands. "Oggy-oggy-oggy!" he sang out, as he jabbed a huge pointing finger into the air.

"Oi! Oi! Oi!" the crowd called back, completing the ritual chant.

"Let's play soccer!" yelled Nooth.

Dino blew a loud *Phweeeep!* on his bronze whistle. There was a mighty roar from the crowd . . .

. . . and all around Dug, chaos broke out.

It quickly became clear that the ball was the focus of the contest. Both teams of men began to chase enthusiastically around after it, kicking it back and forth to each another. Dug dashed randomly around the grass, doing his very best to stay out of harm's way. The gruff man who had stopped him in the corridor shouted over to him, frowning.

"Hugelgraber! What are you doing?" He gestured urgently toward one end of the arena. "Get in the goal!"

Dug was desperate not to give himself away. He must try to act like Hugelgraber would. He hurried toward the white, netted thing his scowling teammate had pointed to.

He was finding it very difficult to run in Hugelgraber's strange foot-coverings. Dug had never worn cleats, or footwear of any kind. He had no idea that he had put them on the wrong feet.

As he stumbled toward the goalmouth, he tripped over his own feet. He took a sprawling dive, and by sheer luck, blocked a fierce shot with his backside.

Dug picked himself up. He was terrified to see several of the opposing team charging toward him. The ball was beside him.

"Pick it up!" he heard a teammate yell. "Pick it up!"

Dug did as he was told. He snatched up the ball. To his great relief, the other players immediately began to move away from him, spreading out.

"To me, to me!" called Mr. Magnificent from some distance away. Dug obediently set off across the grass to carry the ball to him. "What?" cried his dismayed teammate. "No! Put it down! Put it down!" But it was too late.

"Handball!" bellowed the opposition players.

Referee Dino gave a blast on his whistle. "Free kick!" he declared.

Dug's handsome teammate glared at him in disbelief. "Hugelgraber!" he snarled. "Just get in the game!"

Dug was clearly doing everything wrong. He stumbled miserably back toward the goal, wondering how long it would be before he blew his cover.

The free kick came powering straight at him. It smashed into his helmet, and rebounded high into the air.

The blow left Dug dazed. He lifted his head dizzily to look up at the ball spinning in the air above. It began to fall back towards him.

"Just kick it!" screamed the home fans.

Then, suddenly, as he stared at the falling ball, Dug experienced a strange moment of revelation. Time seemed to slow. The noise around him faded.

Images flashed across his mind's eye. He saw the cave paintings back in the Tribe's valley settlement, with their small, round, mysterious objects that Bobnar thought were badly drawn rabbits.

In a rush of understanding, Dug knew why the ball seemed so familiar. He knew what his ancestors were doing in the ancient paintings. They were playing this game, this so-called "soccer!"

Dug snapped back to the here-and-now. The ball was still dropping toward him. The other team's players were bearing down on him.

"KICK IT!" yelled the crowd.

So Dug kicked it. But it wasn't just any old kick. It was as if Dug were seized by some remarkable soccer instinct. Without thinking, he performed an acrobatic overhead kick.

Unfortunately, he fluffed it.

The miskicked ball swerved wildly through the air . . .

. . . into the back of Dug's own net.

The crowd erupted. The angry groans and jeers of the home fans drowned out the joyful whoops of the few visiting supporters.

Up in his private box, Lord Nooth had missed Dug's acrobatic own goal. He was too busy gloating

over the day's takings, a great pile of bronze schnookels that had just been poured into a box beside him. Nooth wasn't really interested in soccer. It was the money it made for him that he adored.

The sudden explosion of crowd noise brought him out of his trance.

"What?"

Spotting the ball in the back of the net, he hastily tried to cover his lapse of attention. "Ah, yes . . . GOAL!" he declared over the din.

Down in the arena, Dug had been mobbed by the other team's players. To his alarm, they seemed determined to hug and kiss him as part of their energetic goal celebrations.

When Dug finally managed to break free, it was only to be confronted by an angry-looking Mr. Magnificent.

"You idiot!" he growled, glowering at Dug. "You just scored an own goal, Hugelgraber!"

Before Dug could reply, a sudden angry yell made his heart sink.

"Stop the match! He's not me!"

It was the man whose clothes Dug had swiped in the changing room—the real Hugelgraber. He

was standing at the edge of the field, still stark naked. Only the corner flag saved his blushes. He was pointing furiously at Dug.

It looked like the game was up.

CHAPTER FIVE

A LATE CHALLENGE

Mr. Magnificent looked from Dug to his naked teammate and back again. His perfect blue eyes narrowed. He grabbed Dug's helmet, and tugged it off.

There were gasps of surprise from all around the arena as the shocked crowd took in Dug's true identity. Up in his private box, Lord Nooth sprang to his feet in outrage.

"A caveman?" he roared in disbelief.

"A CAVEMAN!" echoed the appalled crowd.

"Playing the Sacred Game?" hissed Nooth with cold fury. "Seize him!" he commanded. "Bring him here!"

Dug tried to make a run for it, but was quickly grabbed by guards. They dragged him across the field into the shadow of Nooth's box. Nooth glared angrily down at him. He pointed an accusing and colossal finger.

"How dare you—"

Nooth broke off. His giant-sized foam fingers were rather spoiling the desired effect. He cast them aside, then tried his menacing glare-and-point routine again.

"How dare you set foot on our hallowed ground?"

Dug looked around at the many disapproving faces scowling down at him. He knew he was in a bad spot. But frightened as he was, he was not about to let a bully like Nooth treat him like dirt. He dug deep for some courage.

"You took our ground!" he told the Bronze leader defiantly. "Our home!"

Nooth smirked nastily. "Oh, that," he said, as if his invasion of the Valley had been a trifling matter. "You have no home," he told Dug, with a mocking sneer. "Your kind are finished on this earth."

He gestured impatiently to the guards holding Dug.

"Take him away and kill him," he ordered. "Slowly!"

Nooth's men knew to obey his every word, or face the consequences. They began dragging Dug toward the arena exit as slowly as they could.

"No, you idiots!" snapped Nooth, red-faced. "I mean take him away at normal speed and kill him slowly!"

The guards hastily accelerated the pace of Dug's removal.

"Now . . . get on with the match!" Nooth ordered Dino and the players.

Dug, however, was not done yet. As the guards dragged him away, the sight of the two crossed spears brought the build up to the match flashing back. Words echoed in his mind: *We challenge the champions*. He thought again of the cave paintings of his ancestors. If they could play soccer . . .

"Wait!" he protested, struggling to get free. "WAIT!"

With one last effort, he managed to squirm out of the guards' grip. He snatched a corner flag, and went sprinting back out across the grass. He intercepted the ball, and speared it with the flag's spike.

Bang!

Having regained the attention of the crowd, Dug played his last card.

"WE CHALLENGE THE CHAMPIONS!" he yelled, trying to appear as bold as he could.

For the second time, gasps rippled around the arena. A shocked hush fell.

"What did you say?" sneered Lord Nooth. He looked down at Dug in amused disbelief.

"He said," Dino called up from below, "WE CHALLENGE THE—"

Nooth cut his assistant off impatiently. "I heard what he said!"

Dug tried to hold his nerve. "If we win," he told Nooth, "we get to keep our Valley. You have to leave my tribe in peace."

Nooth let out a scornful laugh. "You think you can beat us at soccer?" He smirked. "A match between the Bronze and the brutes." He shook his head. "What a ridiculous idea!"

Mr. Magnificent was still glaring at Dug. "Such a contest would bring the Sacred Game into disrepute!" he snarled.

"Sacrilege!" added Dino disapprovingly. "Only the common masses would flock to see such a vulgar spectacle."

As these last words of Dino's sank in, a change came over Lord Nooth's expression. "Flock, you say?" he murmured, thoughtfully. "The masses, eh? You think so?" He looked to the brimming box of schnookels nearby, and a sly smile spread across his face. "Hmmmm . . ."

To the scheming, money-loving Nooth, Dug's "ridiculous idea" was beginning to look less ridiculous by the second.

As things turned out, Dug had more trouble persuading his own leader than Lord Nooth to accept his bold idea.

Following Nooth's public acceptance of his challenge, Dug was released, and he made the trek back to the Badlands as fast as his legs would carry him. His reunion with the Tribe was a joyful one. Bobnar and the others had feared the worst after his disappearance. And no one was happier to see him than Hognob.

It was impossible, however, for the Tribe to stay in high spirits for long. Their situation was grim. The Bronze invaders were still occupying the Valley.

They had built a high fence around it, to keep out "primitives." The Tribe were outcasts now, forced to survive in the deadly territory of the Badlands. They were hungry, tired, and scared.

Dug was determined to give them hope. He had brought it back with him from the Bronze City, in the form of a soccer ball, and a copy of the program from his first ever match. He wasted no time in telling his friends his plan.

"Soccer," he told them, as they huddled together in their makeshift Badlands camp. "That's how we get our Valley back."

"Soccer?" said Bobnar, frowning. "What's 'soccer'?"

Dug passed around the match program. It was full of etchings of the Bronze team in action. His friends flicked through its pages in wide-eyed wonder.

"It's this amazing game, Chief!" Dug explained. "And the leader of the Bronze people says that if we play this game, and beat them at it—"

"Ooh, nice tight shorts!" interrupted Magma, admiring a player picture.

"Aw, Mom . . . please!" groaned Treebor, looking deeply embarrassed.

"If we beat them at it," Dug went on, "we can have our Valley back!"

At this, the Tribe looked overjoyed.

"That's what we want!" cried Treebor.

Only Bobnar looked doubtful. "And if we don't beat them?" he asked.

Dug became a little sheepish.

"Then Nooth said . . . he said we'll spend the rest of our miserable lives working down the mine."

Barry took this badly. "Noooooooooooo!" he wailed. Then his look of terror gave way to a puzzled frown. "What's a mine?" he asked Thongo.

Bobnar was considering Dug's plan. He looked unconvinced.

"Dug," he said wearily. "We're a rabbit-hunting tribe. We've never even played this game!"

"But that's just it!" cried Dug. "We did . . . once. The cave paintings back in our Valley, they're pictures of our ancestors playing soccer!" He looked eagerly around the group. "Our ancestors were mighty soccer players!"

The others needed a few moments to take in this bombshell.

"Champions!" murmured an awestruck Asbo, speaking for them all.

"So, if they did it, surely we can do it!" Dug concluded triumphantly.

Bobnar still wasn't persuaded. "I don't see that this changes anything, Dug," he said. "It's just too risky."

The others, however, were behind Dug's plan.

"Come on, Chief! We can do it!" urged Gravelle.

"I wanna play soccer!" insisted Asbo. "I wanna play now! Now!"

"Waiyaiwecannalooosssmaaan!" agreed Eemak.

"NO!" said Bobnar firmly, putting his foot down for once.

The others looked glum. With long faces and slumped shoulders, they turned and began to slope away.

"Fine. Don't worry about us," muttered Treebor. "We'll just stay here and eat dinosaur bones all day."

"Yeah, we'll be okay," said Asbo, miserably. "We'll just die a slow and lingering death in the Badlands."

"Come on, Chief!" pleaded Dug. He could tell that their soft-hearted old leader was weakening.

With a heavy sigh, Bobnar gave in. "Look . . . all right!" he said. The others turned eagerly back to

him. "We'll give this 'soccer' idea a try. See how it goes. But no promises!"

"Thank you, Chief!" beamed Dug. His eyes filled with steely determination. "The match will be held at the next full moon," he told the others. "All we have to do is win. Then we go back to the Valley!"

As his friends let out an enthusiastic cheer, Dug's words echoed in his mind. *All we have to do is win.* He felt a rush of confidence. For a tribe with such soccer talent in their blood, how hard could that be?

CHAPTER SIX

TRIBE IN TRAINING

It was an excited and enthusiastic Tribe that gathered the next morning for their very first soccer training session.

Dug had been up since sunrise getting things ready. He had chosen the least dangerous part of Badlands terrain he could find nearby, and set to work turning it into a basic playing field. With Hognob's help, he had collected enough dinosaur bones to build a pair of makeshift goals. For field markings, they had laid out lines of large shells. These weren't ideal, as some still had fierce Badlands crabs living inside them and had a tendency to move around every now and then. But it was the best they could manage with what was on hand.

Now, as the rest of the Tribe looked admiringly at what he and Hognob had put together, Dug felt proud of their handiwork.

"Okay!" barked Bobnar, taking charge. "Line up, everybody!"

The Tribe shuffled eagerly into a single row in front of Bobnar and Dug. Bobnar noticed Hognob joining the lineup. He raised his bushy eyebrows. "Are hogs supposed to play soccer?" he asked Dug.

Dug looked awkward. "Erm, probably not, no. Sorry, Hognob."

With a sulky look, Hognob slunk out of the line.

"All yours, Dug," said Bobnar, stepping back to watch.

"Thanks, Chief. Right. So . . ." Dug looked at his friends' eager faces. Where should he start? He gestured to the marked-out area. "This is a 'soccer field,'" he began, in his best one-step-at-a-time teaching style. "Here, we play soccer."

The Tribe stared at him with blank faces. There was some puzzled muttering. Bobnar, looking on, spoke for them.

"Uh . . . how, Dug?" he asked.

Dug pressed on. He held up the ball. "This is a soccer ball," he explained. "One team tries to kick the ball in this 'goal.'" He pointed to the nearest dinosaur-bone goal.

Turning their heads to look, the Tribe let out a collective, "Oooooo!"

"And the other team tries to kick the ball in *that* 'goal.'" Dug pointed again.

"Aaaaahhh!" murmured the others, fascinated, as they took this in.

Barry was already looking lost. "Soccer sounds hard," he complained.

Treebor put his hand up. "What happens if you do kick the ball in the goal?" he asked.

Dug thought back to his experience in the Bronze City. "If you kick the ball in a goal," he replied, "other men hug and kiss you."

This met with mixed reactions. To Treebor's obvious embarrassment, Magma suddenly looked a lot more interested. "Let's get started!" she said enthusiastically.

"That's the spirit, Magma!" beamed Dug. "All right, then . . ." He placed the ball at Magma's feet, then moved back a little. "I'll try to take the ball from you, and you try to stop me, okay?"

Dug ran at Magma. Without hesitation, she knocked him flat on his back with a fearsome right hook. The rest of the Tribe showed their approval.

"Good one, Magma!"

"That's the way!"

"Nice one, Mom!"

"Soccer's awesome!" enthused Asbo, who was liking the look of this strange new game.

Only Bobnar seemed to sense that Magma might have misunderstood. "Surely you can't hit other players?" He frowned.

Dug was still recovering. "No," he said feebly, sitting up and rubbing his jaw. "You're supposed to attack the ball."

In a heartbeat, the entire Tribe snatched up their clubs and charged wildly toward the soccer ball.

"No! No-no-no!" shrieked Dug. "Not that kind of attack! Not with weapons!"

The Tribe stopped in their tracks. Asbo looked at Dug in confusion. "Just fists?" he said.

"No!" insisted Dug. "No fighting at all!"

Shoulders sagged and mouths drooped. This was clearly a major disappointment to all. "Where's the fun in that?" complained Magma, whose earlier enthusiasm was fading fast.

Dug let out a sigh. So far, training was not going as smoothly as he'd hoped.

As the morning wore on, things only got worse. Despite their soccer-playing ancestry, the Tribe seemed unable to pick up even the most basic of skills.

Dug had them take turns trying a simple penalty shot first. This, he thought, would be a good way to practice just kicking the ball. He persuaded a reluctant Treebor to go stand in the goal.

Thongo missed the ball completely, slipped, and went sliding into the goal himself. Magma gave the ball a mighty kick . . . backwards, straight into poor Eemak's stomach. Only Asbo made proper contact, and his shot was so wildly off target, the ball flew over the fence, into the Valley.

Dug hurried off to retrieve the ball, which was their only one. He smiled sweetly at the Bronze guard on the other side of the fence.

"Can we have our ball back, please?"

The guard grumpily obliged. Dug headed back with the ball to rejoin the others, wondering if passing practice might be a better way to start.

A training session was taking place in the Bronze City, too. The awesome players of Real Bronzio, golden-haired Mr. Magnificent and his talented teammates, were fine-tuning their soccer skills. They passed, dribbled, and juggled the ball with the style and ease of experts.

Lord Nooth watched smugly from his private apartment, which overlooked the stadium. His assistant, Dino, was with him.

"This soccer match between the Stone Age and the Bronze world—it's perfect!" said Nooth, grinning. He was already imagining the riches that the match would bring in.

Dino, however, looked a little anxious.

"What if the queen finds out, Your Premiership?" he asked.

The Bronze realm's formidable monarch, Queen Oofeefa, ruled with a firm hand and an eagle eye. Her seat of power, however, was some distance from the city.

"Pah! The old crow doesn't know what goes on out here!" said Nooth. He was eager to avoid the queen's interference. She was sure to disapprove of his cunning schnookel-making scheme.

But the "old crow" was not as out of touch as Nooth hoped.

A loud *Squawk!* behind him made him jump. A royal message-bird was sitting on the windowsill. It hopped into the room, and began to strut back and forth on Nooth's desk in a regal manner.

"I've heard about the match, Nooth!" said the bird, in a perfect imitation of Queen Oofeefa's haughty voice. It stopped, and glared at Nooth. "You IDIOT!" it snapped. "Imagine if we lost!"

The bird's impersonation of the queen was uncanny. Both Nooth and Dino were finding it more than a little unsettling.

"We . . . we won't—" stammered Nooth.

"YOU'D BETTER NOT!" bellowed the bird, continuing its recorded message. It grabbed Nooth by his lapels. "I'm warning you, Nooth. I won't have the mighty Bronze Age brought to its knees by a bunch of cavemen!"

Still in character, the bird gave Nooth's nose a painful twist. Then, with another *Squawk!*, it hopped onto the windowsill, its message complete.

"Silly old bat," muttered Nooth, rubbing his sore nose. "How dare she talk to me like that?"

"Silly old bat. How dare she talk to me like that?" echoed the bird, in Nooth's voice. "Delivering message!" it squawked, and flew off before Nooth could stop it.

Nooth scowled after the bird, wishing he had held his tongue. Queen Oofeefa's threatening words had spoiled his good mood. They had not, however, shaken his faith in his plan. Let the cavemen do their worst, he thought. They were no match for the mighty Real Bronzio.

Back in the Badlands, the Tribe were indeed doing their worst.

Passing practice was going no better than shooting had. No matter how often Dug told them not to, his friends insisted on running around in one big pack, chasing the ball. It didn't help that Grubup kept trying to capture and eat it.

By the end of the first day's training, the Tribe had made no progress whatsoever, and had lost all their enthusiasm. Even Dug was feeling flat.

It was not in Dug's nature, however, to stay down for long. It was bound to take a little time

for things to come together, he told himself. By the next morning, he was back to his usual upbeat self.

"Rise and shine!" he told the others cheerily, as he woke them early with a bucketful of cold water. "Training time!"

The second training session went as badly as the first.

So did the third.

And the fourth.

As the days went by, and the moon grew fuller, the Tribe remained as hopeless at soccer as ever. It was all Dug could do to hold on to his belief that they would, eventually, get the hang of it.

Not everybody had his faith. When Bobnar came to see how things were going at the umpteenth session, his heart sank.

"Stop bunching! Less bunching," Dug yelled at the others, who were lumbering about after the ball in one big rabble. "To him! To her! Kick it to each other more!"

Barry was sitting out the session in a sulk. Soccer, as far as he was concerned, was simply too hard.

Hognob, on the other hand, kept trying to

sneak in on the action, despite repeated reminders of the no-hogs-allowed rule.

"My toe hurts!" whined Gravelle, who had complained of more injuries in recent days than Bobnar could count.

Eemak, meanwhile, had suffered a genuine injury. Purple-faced, he clutched the vulnerable area that Magma had just kicked.

"When I said 'free kick,'" Dug told Magma wearily, "I meant of the ball!"

Elsewhere, Treebor was cowering and trembling. Several of the line marker crabs were closing in on him. He gave a scream of terror and fled.

Bobnar took it all in with a grim expression. It was a shambles.

And what happened next put an end to training altogether.

Grubup had gone wandering off moments earlier, looking for something to eat, as always. He had spotted a tasty-looking wild duck nearby. It was only when he hurled a rock at it that he realized it was much, much bigger than he had first thought. Like most Badlands wildlife it was, in fact, monstrous.

The tyrannosaur-sized duck came stomping angrily after Grubup, who ran for his life, back toward the training ground.

"DUCK!" he screamed to the Tribe in warning.

His friends ducked down, looking up anxiously for the danger.

"No!" yelled the wide-eyed Grubup, pointing. "DUCK!"

The others saw the monstrous mallard charging their way, and fled.

In the chase that followed, the rampaging creature wrecked the training ground. Worst of all, it stomped on the soccer ball, bursting it. Without a ball to play with, further practices were impossible.

It was a glum, battered, and weary group who slumped around the campfire that night. Dug sat alone, a little way off, looking out over the Valley below. Bobnar came to talk to him.

"Dug, it's time to give up this soccer fantasy," said Bobnar quietly. He gestured to the others. "For their sake. They're just not capable of it."

Dug continued to gaze wistfully at his old home. "Don't you miss the Valley, Chief?" he asked.

"The Valley's gone now," replied Bobnar. "And we're better off here in the Badlands than slaving down in some mine. At least we're still together. We're still a tribe."

Dug, however, was not ready to quit. "But our ancestors played soccer. We know they did!" he insisted. "I still believe we can do this!"

"With what?" For once, Bobnar ran out of patience. "You don't even have a ball to play with!" he said hotly. "It's over!"

As Bobnar returned to the campfire, Dug looked up at the night sky. It would be a few days until the moon was full.

"It isn't over," he told himself. "There's still time."

He just needed to get his hands on another ball, so that the Tribe could get back to training. And Dug knew exactly where to find one.

CHAPTER SEVEN

GOONA HITS THE SPOT

Breaking into the Bronze City at night wasn't easy. The city was well protected. Armed guards manned its main gateway and patrolled its perimeter fence. Dug had to use all his stealth and agility, not to mention a rope with a hook made of elk antlers, to get past its defenses.

Hognob, his faithful friend, had of course come with him. He sneaked in with rather less fuss, thanks to a handy cat flap.

Once inside the city, the two friends crept silently through its dark, deserted streets. When they reached the mighty temple-like stadium, they found its entrance locked and guarded. High on one of its looming sides, however, a small window was ajar.

A way in.

"Okay, Hognob," whispered Dug, as he prepared to use his antler grappling hook once more. "Let's go get some balls!" This was what they had made the moonlit trek from the Badlands for. Inside the soccer stadium they would find what they needed, Dug was sure.

After a good deal of scrabbling and hauling, they tumbled in through the high window, into a plush, luxuriously furnished room. They were in Lord Nooth's private apartment! An opening in the far wall led out onto a balcony—Nooth's VIP box, overlooking the great arena itself.

"You stay here, Hognob," whispered Dug. He hurried to the balcony and out into the stands. He glanced back as he began making his way down the tiers of seating. "I don't want to attract attention . . . *wooaaah!*"

Dug had failed to notice a bright yellow CAUTION sign perched on a damaged step. He tripped over it, and went tumbling down the rows of seats. He clattered and crashed all the way down to the ground level, where he landed in a messy heap. As

he sat up, dazed, the sign came bouncing down the stands after him and clonked him hard on his head.

It took Dug a moment or two to recover from his tumble. He was suddenly aware that he was not alone in the arena. There was someone moving around on the unlit field. Dug hurriedly took cover behind a stand. Peering out cautiously, he watched the stranger out on the grass.

As the figure moved from shadow into moonlight, Dug saw to his surprise that it was the blonde-haired girl from the market stall, the one who had told him off for bumping into her pans. She was kicking a ball around, alone. She was muttering her own running commentary as she played.

"And the exciting new signing picks the ball up in the center circle. She beats one, nutmegs another . . ."

Dug watched, fascinated, as the girl dribbled the soccer ball skillfully across the grass. Her ball control was superb. She looped the ball into the air with a clever flick, then controlled it beautifully as it came back down.

"She lobs it neatly over the big fullback. She's going all the way . . . She shoots . . ."

Her fierce, curling shot went rocketing into the back of the net.

"She scores! Yeah! The crowd goes wild! GOOOAL!"

Dug was spellbound by the Bronze Age girl and her extraordinary skill. He moved to get a better view and trod on the CAUTION sign. It made a loud crunching noise.

The girl froze. Dug ducked out of sight as she turned sharply to stare in his direction. A few seconds passed in silence. Nothing happened. Dug took a cautious peek.

Thwapp!

A perfectly aimed soccer ball hit him hard on the forehead. The blow knocked him flat on his back, out cold.

When he came to a few seconds later, he found the Bronze girl standing over him. She had a look of surprise on her face.

"Hey, you're that crazy caveman guy!" she said.

"The angry . . . pan . . . girl," murmured Dug blearily.

"What are you doing here, caveman?" demanded the girl, keeping her voice low. "This is the Sacred Turf! No one's allowed!"

"Balls," said Dug, trying to clear his head. "I need balls."

The girl raised her eyebrows. "You came all this way and broke into the stadium just to find some balls?" She looked almost impressed. "Wow. You're pretty brave, caveman. And stupid. Actually more stupid than brave, really."

"Thanks," said Dug, uncertainly.

The girl grinned at him. "I'm Goona, by the way," she said.

Her smile's pretty, thought Dug and immediately he felt his face redden.

"Dug," he said, grinning back bashfully.

Goona grabbed his hand to help him up.

"If it's balls you're after, I can help," she hissed. "Come on!"

She quickly led Dug to a door at one side of the darkened arena and along a gloomy corridor. Moments later, they were inside the home team's clubhouse. Its storage room was crammed with soccer equipment.

Goona found a ball net. Together, she and Dug hastily began filling it with soccer balls.

"I envy you," Goona told Dug as she shoved another ball into the net.

"Me?" frowned Dug.

"Having the chance to play on that field," said Goona with a dreamy look in her eyes. "The Sacred Turf. In front of thousands of fans . . ."

"Maybe you will one day," said Dug encouragingly. From what he had seen of Goona's skills, she was certainly good enough.

Goona gave him a look.

"You think they let girls play for Real Bronzio?" She shook her head. "You really are crazy. Why do you think I sneak in here?"

Before Dug could reply, a beam of light suddenly shone along the corridor. Dug and Goona froze at the sound of approaching footsteps.

"Who is that?" called a suspicious voice. "Who's there?"

It was Dino, Lord Nooth's right-hand man.

"Run!" cried Goona to Dug.

They ran for it, Dug dragging the bulging ball net behind him. Dino came after them, yelling.

"Stop! Thieves!"

Goona found a way to slow Dino down. As she and Dug fled, she tugged loose a net crammed with giant-sized foam fingers. They spilled out, burying Dino. By the time he managed to escape the pile, his head was firmly stuck inside one of the huge hands.

Arena guards came rushing, drawn by Dino's yells. "They went that way!" Dino told them urgently, in a muffled voice.

The puzzled guards looked straight upward, following the giant pointing finger on Dino's head.

"NO!" raged Dino. He bent over to aim the finger in the direction of the fleeing intruders. "That way!"

By now, Dug and Goona had made it back out into the arena. But as they sprinted across the pitch, the guards came after them.

"Wait!" Goona told Dug. "Give me those, quick!" She snatched the ball net, and emptied out several balls. Turning to face the pursuing guards, she quickly struck each ball in turn, free-kick style.

Every kick found its target. One by one, the guards went down, flat on their backs, as Goona's soccer ball missiles took them out. Dug watched, amazed, as she floored the last two guards with a single ball.

"You're really good!" he told her warmly.

Goona smiled. "Thanks. I do a lot of practice."

Dug's mind was racing. He thought of Goona's

impressive soccer skills, and of how she dreamed of playing on the Sacred Turf, and of how badly the Tribe's training had been going . . .

His eyes shone as he beamed at Goona.

"I think I've just had a great idea," he said.

CHAPTER EIGHT

PIG TROUBLE

While Dug and Goona were stealing balls and dodging guards, Hognob was having an adventure of his own.

Dug's clumsy tumble down the stadium seating had left his best friend in a rather sticky situation. The noise of his fall had drawn unwelcome attention. Before Hognob could go to Dug's aid, he froze at the sound of a suspicious voice.

"What's all that crashing around out there?"

The voice came from a room next to the one Hognob and Dug had broken into. Hognob recognized it at once. It belonged to the man who had led the attack on his beloved valley home.

"Is that you, Stefano?" demanded Nooth impatiently. "Stop messing around and get in here with those firm hands of yours!"

Hognob's hoggy mind raced. If he made a run for it, Lord Nooth was sure to realize there were intruders at large, and call for the guards. Dug would almost certainly be captured.

There was only one answer. Hognob had to bluff, and buy his best friend some time. He trotted over to the door to the next room, and cautiously slipped through.

The room beyond was Lord Nooth's private spa. It was clouded with steam and a luxurious bronze bath stood at its center. Nooth was relaxing in the bubble-frothed water, reading a newspaper. He had his back to the door. Hearing someone enter, he barked another impatient command.

"Come on, Stefano! It's time for my massage."

The word "massage" meant little to Hognob. His idea of pampering was a good old roll in the mud. He was, however, far smarter than the average hog. He noticed a table full of creams and lotions, and remembered Nooth's talk of "firm hands." He put two and two together.

Nervously fumbling with one of the bottles, he managed to smear his trotters with massage oil, after squirting a fair bit in his eye.

"Come on, chop-chop!" snapped Nooth. "I haven't got all day."

Hognob took the plunge. Approaching from behind, he laid his oily trotters on Nooth's bare shoulders. He began to rub and squeeze them, hoping he had more or less the right idea. From Nooth's reaction, it seemed he had.

"Aaaaahhhh, yesssss . . ." sighed the Bronze leader in satisfaction. "That's good! I need this, Stefano. Don't go easy on me. My tendons are like ropes. You can go the whole hog."

Hognob tensed. For a moment, he feared he had been discovered. But Nooth seemed more than happy for him to continue.

The truth was that Lord Nooth was feeling especially in need of a little stress relief. The angry message that Queen Oofeefa had sent him had left him rather anxious and annoyed.

Now, however, as Hognob's trotters did their soothing work, Nooth's cares dissolved away. He felt only smug satisfaction with the cleverness of his latest scheme. The match against the primitives would really bring in the bronze. His coin chests would soon be brimming with beautiful schnookels.

"Mmmmm . . ." he sighed contentedly. "I don't know what the queen is worrying about. I mean, we all know what losers cavemen are. Those Stone Age dolts couldn't beat their own grandmothers."

These words did not go down well with Hognob. Thinking of Dug, he tried to keep his temper. His kneading and slapping of Nooth's flesh, however, became rather more enthusiastic.

"Brainless goons," Nooth went on. "Gormless half-wits. Ignorant—*Owwww!*" Nooth gave a cry of pain as Hognob's increasingly furious massaging become too rough to bear. "Stefano! Not so ham-fisted!" Nooth shrugged Hognob's trotters away irritably. "In fact, enough massage. How about some relaxing music instead?" He gestured over his shoulder to a corner of the room where a large bronze harp stood.

Hognob looked at the harp in dismay. Now what? He didn't seem to have much choice. He had to keep up the deception, for Dug's sake.

He trotted quickly over to the harp and, after a brief hesitation, tried a few experimental plucks at its strings.

Twang-twoing-twing!

It sounded awful. Trotters weren't made for harp-plucking.

Suddenly, Hognob caught the sound of yelling. It was coming from the stadium. It sounded like angry guards. Hognob knew he must prevent Lord Nooth from hearing. He hastily began making as much noise as possible. Strumming wildly on the harp, he howled a tuneless, ear-splitting "melody."

Nooth winced and covered his ears. "Agghhh! What on earth's gotten into you tonight, Stefano?" He turned angrily to scowl at his man.

Only it wasn't his man. It wasn't a man at all.

"Stefano?"

As Nooth stared at Hognob, the real Stefano came striding into the spa room, a towel over his arm.

"Yes, sire?" he said. Then his eyes, too, fixed on Hognob.

Nooth's brain finally grasped the alarming truth. He let out a horrified shriek. Stefano shrieked louder. Hognob joined in for good measure.

Nooth was silenced a moment later. A soccer ball crashed through one of the spa room's windows.

It hit Nooth hard on the head, knocking him over. He disappeared beneath his bathwater.

To Hognob's surprise and relief, Dug burst in through the broken window. A blonde-haired girl was right behind him.

"Hognob!" cried Dug, hurriedly grabbing his best friend. "Hognob, meet Goona!" he beamed. "Goona, Hognob."

The girl smiled. "Hi, Hognob!"

Stefano looked on in bewilderment. Before he knew what was happening, the three strangers were making their escape. With Dug clutching the end of an unraveling toilet paper roll, they leaped from another window and swung down to the ground outside. Within seconds, they had vanished into the night.

Lord Nooth resurfaced from his bathwater, spluttering and gasping for air. Stefano hurried to his aid.

"Sire, are you all right?"

The fuming, foam-covered Governor glared at his servant in pure fury.

"Of course I'm not all right, you harp-playing herbert!" he roared. "I've just been massaged by a pig!"

CHAPTER NINE

BALL SKILLS, BADLANDS STYLE!

When Dug woke the Tribe early the next morning, with the usual bucketful of water, he was a different caveman from the evening before. The sparkle was back in his eyes.

"Wake up, everyone!" he said eagerly. "I want you all to meet someone!"

The others rose and followed him reluctantly, still half asleep. Out on the duck-wrecked training ground, a stranger was playing with a soccer ball. It was a girl. From her strange clothing, it was clear she was from the same Bronze tribe as the Valley's invaders.

Her ball skills were amazing. The Tribe had never seen keepy-uppy before. They watched, spellbound, as the girl juggled the ball with expert touches of her feet, knees, and head. She caught it on the back of her neck, flicked it high, then cooly kept it in the air as she came over to join them.

"This is Goona," Dug told his friends. "She's a real soccer player. She's going to help us win the game!"

Goona trapped the ball skilfully under one foot. "Hi!" she said, with a cheery smile. "Glad to be on board."

This was Dug's great idea. He had persuaded Goona to come back to the Badlands with him, to help his struggling team, by promising that she could join it. That way, she could live out her own dream. She could play on the Sacred Turf, in front of thousands of yelling fans.

Goona wasted no time in getting down to business.

"So, what formation do you normally play?" she asked.

"Formation?" said Dug.

"Four-four-two or four-three-three?" said

Goona. "Who's your sweeper? Do you man-mark, or play zonally?"

There were blank looks all around.

"We just kick the ball and chase it," said Treebor.

Goona was quickly realizing just what she had taken on. "You think you can beat Real Bronzio by chasing a ball around?" she said. She shook her head. "You guys need to know what you're up against!"

So the Tribe's training began afresh with an introduction to their rivals. Goona had brought her own soccer card collection with her. With its help, she took the Tribe through the Real Bronzio players one by one.

The first card she laid down showed the handsome golden-haired striker who had given Dug a hard time. "That's Jurgund, the captain," said Goona. "Best goalscorer in the known world. Knows it, too."

Dug also recognized the player on the second card. "Their winger, Lightning Hammer," said Goona. "Never strikes twice in the same place."

She displayed another card, and another.

"Midfield dynamo, Qwik Wun Tu. He can kick faster than you can think . . . Finally, their fullback. No one gets past his tackle . . ."

By the time the complete Real Bronzio squad was laid out before them, the Tribe looked thoroughly disheartened.

"They're like ginormous, giant, soccer-playing . . . giants!" said Asbo.

"The best players bronze can buy," agreed Goona.

"There's no way we can beat such a great team!" groaned Gravelle.

Goona gave her a feisty look. "Well, not if you talk like that, there isn't!" she said. "If you think like losers, then you've already lost."

Dug knew she was right. "What Goona's saying . . ." he told the others, "is that we need to believe in ourselves."

Barry's face lit up. "I believe in my shelves!" he cried, getting entirely the wrong end of the stick, as usual. He had recently built himself a (rather wonky) shelving unit out of dinosaur bones. It was for displaying his collection of stones, and his (badly drawn) portrait of Mr. Rock, his late best friend. He was very proud of it.

"We've got a lot of hard work to do," Goona pressed on. She looked around the Tribe, taking a quick headcount. The others plus her made ten.

"We don't even have a full team. We need one more."

Hognob's ears pricked up. For a moment, he thought he was in luck. His hopes were crushed, however, by the sudden arrival of Bobnar.

"What's going on?" asked the old chief, who had been asleep in his cave. He looked suspiciously at Goona, and at the ball she was holding. "I thought we were done with soccer."

In no time at all, Goona had been introduced to Bobnar, and had appointed him, despite his protests, as the team's final member. In the light of his extreme old age, nearly thirty-two, she assigned him the role of goalkeeper.

"Right, that's settled then!" said Goona, to whom taking charge came naturally. "Now, where are your training facilities?"

"Training facilities?" said Dug. He remembered the impressive range of equipment back in the Real Bronzio clubhouse. He looked glum. "All we've got is . . ." suddenly, a smile lit his face, ". . . the Badlands!" he cried. Dug's eyes shone as they met Goona's.

He had just had another great idea.

As a soccer training facility, the Badlands had it all. It just took a little imagination, which both Dug and Goona had plenty of, to see it.

Who needed cones to practice dribbling around when you had spouting geysers to weave between? What could be more ideal for doing quick-steps across than the giant ribcage of a dinosaur skeleton? What better way was there to make the Tribe move and think fast than by having them do their pass-and-go exercises with a giant man-eating duck on their tail?

In the days that followed Goona's arrival, she and Dug found many ingenious ways to turn the deadly hazards of the Badlands into first-class training activities. Under Goona's expert guidance, the Tribe's soccer skills slowly began to improve. In breaks between exercises, she explained rules and tactics with the help of pebble-players and chalk-drawn diagrams.

Bobnar was doubtful at first. He watched anxiously as the others practiced their passing accuracy perched on floating rock islands in a river

of lava. But he could not deny the progress they were making. Before very long, he was joining in as enthusiastically as the others.

As their skills went from strength to strength, the Tribe began to enjoy themselves. When, for the first time, Dug's friends woke *him* with an early soaking, eager to get started, he knew things were well and truly on the up.

Working together, the Tribe and Goona prepared for the challenge ahead. Dug came up with footwear. Since being driven out into the Badlands, the Tribe had survived largely on giant, just-about-edible caterpillars. The tough, leathery caterpillar skins made ideal soccer cleats. Soon they had made themselves matching uniforms, too. Thongo took on the job of dyeing their shirts red with berry juice.

Even Hognob played his part. His new-found massage skills helped soothe his friends' aching muscles at the end of a hard day's training.

Everything was coming together at last.

After a particularly successful day of training, the Tribe celebrated with a noisy party back at camp. By now, Goona was one of the gang. Thongo had even made her a caveman disguise so that she would look the part at the soccer match. She and the Tribe danced happily around the campfire, playing keepy-uppy even as they partied. Bobnar could hardly believe the progress they had made over such a short period of time.

While the others danced, Dug practiced his overhead kick. He was determined to master it. He gave it another try, but once again he failed to strike the ball cleanly. With a sigh, he hurried off, away from the firelight, to retrieve it.

The ball had come to rest against the foot of the invaders' fence. As Dug approached, he looked out over his much-loved valley below. The moon shining down on it was almost full.

"We'll soon be home!" Dug told himself, happily.

Then his face clouded. He had spotted something down in the Valley. There were lights moving. Lots of flaming torches bobbed and moved near the entrance to Bobnar's cave. What was going on down there?

Dug was too distracted to hear the rustle of movement behind him.

Suddenly, he was plunged into darkness. Someone had slipped a hood over his head. A rough hand stifled his attempt to cry out. Other hands seized hold of him.

Struggle as he might, there was nothing Dug could do to stop himself from being dragged away into the night.

CHAPTER TEN

THE AWFUL TRUTH

Dug had no idea where he was being taken. He stumbled blindly along, guided by the shoving and tugging of rough hands.

"What are you doing?" he protested. "Let me go!"

The hood over his head muffled his cries. His mystery kidnappers only bundled him onward, without a word.

Then, at last, they came to a halt. Dug's hood was whipped off, and he could see once more.

What he saw made his blood boil.

His kidnappers, two Bronze guards, had brought him to the Valley cave that used to belong to Bobnar.

Dug looked around in horror. The chief's old home had been wrecked. It was now the main entrance to Lord Nooth's freshly dug bronze mine.

What maddened Dug most was the sight of Nooth himself. He was relaxing in Bobnar's hammock, grinning smugly. Dug glared at him, struggling to get free of his guards' grip.

"Calm down, caveman!" said Nooth mockingly. He swung himself out of Bobnar's bed. "I thought you might like to see our new mine. After all, you will soon be digging lots of bronze out of it."

Dug was defiant. He thought of how much the Tribe's soccer had improved, thanks to Goona. They would soon wipe the smug smile off Nooth's face.

"We're not going down any mine, mammoth-mouth!" growled Dug.

"Ah, yes," said Nooth, still smirking. "Because the skills of your ancestors are in your blood. Is that right?"

Dug looked taken aback. "You . . . you know about them?" he stammered.

Dug had assumed Nooth had no idea about the Tribe's soccer-playing ancestry. They had only just discovered it themselves.

Lord Nooth's unpleasant grin widened. "Bronze isn't all we found down here," he said slyly.

Nooth meant the ancient paintings, Dug supposed. But if Nooth had discovered that the Tribe had soccer in their blood, why did he not seem concerned?

In fact, when Nooth's mining team had first told him of the cave paintings, he had been very concerned. The revelation that the cavemen's ancestors had played the Sacred Game had come as a nasty shock. It suggested a Stone Age team might, after all, be a match for Real Bronzio. To make matters worse, Queen Oofeefa had somehow learned of the worrying discovery. She had sent her royal message-bird to speak to Nooth again. Her angry recorded message made it all too clear that his neck was on the line.

Then, to Nooth's great relief, his miners had brought fresh news. As they dug deeper, they had made another discovery. This time, what they had found washed all his worries away . . .

Lord Nooth crossed to one wall of Bobnar's cave, in which an opening had been newly mined. It was sealed with a heavy bronze door. Nooth pulled a lever, and the door ground slowly open. Beyond it, a dark tunnel led steeply downward. Nooth took a blazing torch from a bracket on the cave wall. Then, to Dug's surprise, he signaled for the guards to release him.

"Come with me, caveman," said Nooth, with another sly smile. "There's something I'd like to show you."

Nooth's "something" was a dark, damp cavern deep underground.

Dug cautiously followed his enemy down into the great, gloomy chamber. He could see by the flickering light of Nooth's torch that its rock walls were decorated with primitive pictures.

"More cave paintings?" said Dug, frowning.

"Yes," replied Nooth. "But these ones tell the whole story."

He held his torch close to the arching cave wall. These paintings, unlike the ones Dug had looked at many times before, were vivid and unfaded. The ones nearest the cave entrance showed a group of hairy primitives kicking around what looked like a ball of rock.

UNLIKELY HEROES

DUG

DUG

The big-hearted hero and star player of the Tribe! He's a can-do caveman and is full of early-man enthusiasm. Dug believes in his friends and is brimming with ambition! He also possesses some smooth Stone Age skills!

HOGNOB

Hognob is Dug's Stone Age pet and devoted friend. Hognob will do anything for his best friend and is protective and trustworthy. He's not much of a talker, but he gets his point across with a well-placed growl!

SIDEKICK-ER

HOGNOB

MEET THE TRIBE

GRAVELLE

EEMAK

TREEBOR

BARRY AND MR. ROCK

BOBNAR

A rock-solid team who will stick together no matter what. This Brutish team of misfits has friendship on their side as they line up ready for kick-off!

THE TRIBE

MAGMA

THONGO

GRUBUP

DUG   **HOGNOB**

ASBO

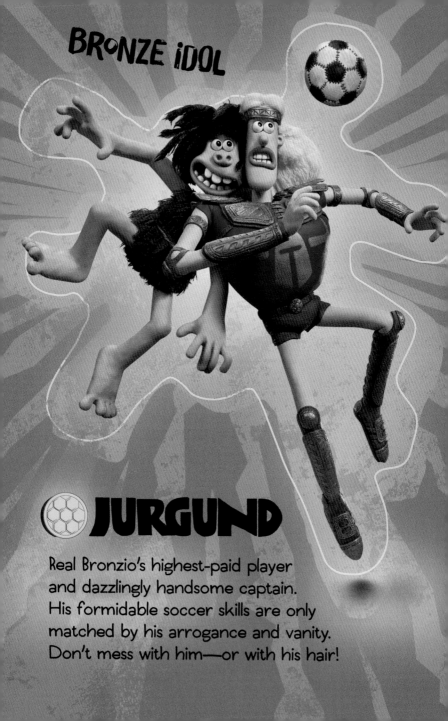

BRONZE IDOL

⬡ JURGUND

Real Bronzio's highest-paid player
and dazzlingly handsome captain.
His formidable soccer skills are only
matched by his arrogance and vanity.
Don't mess with him—or with his hair!

GOONA

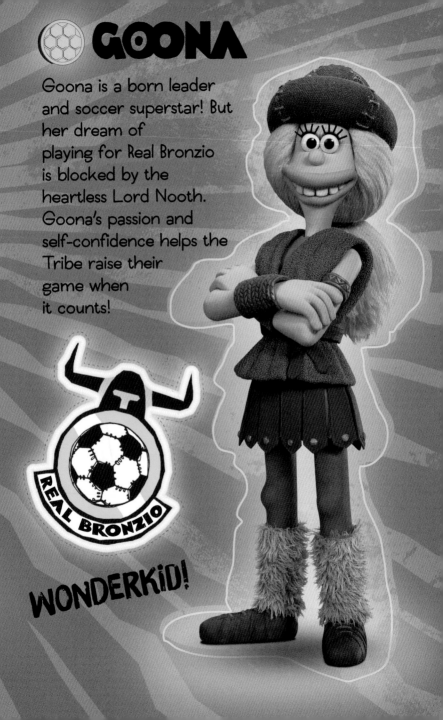

Goona is a born leader and soccer superstar! But her dream of playing for Real Bronzio is blocked by the heartless Lord Nooth. Goona's passion and self-confidence helps the Tribe raise their game when it counts!

REAL BRONZIO

WONDERKID!

LORD NOOTH

The pompous governor of Bronze City and ruthless manager of their elite football team, Real Bronzio. The only thing he loves more than himself is . . . MONEY, and lots of it!

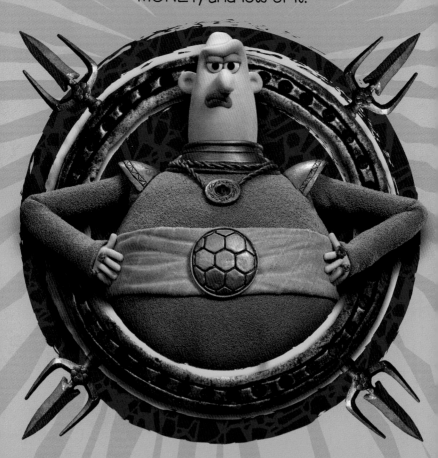

"You see, your ancestors didn't just play soccer," said Nooth. "They invented the game!"

As Nooth moved along the wall, further into the cave, his torch illuminated the story told by the paintings. The next images showed groups of figures arriving to take on Dug's soccer player ancestors.

"You even taught other tribes how to play," Nooth went on. "But you had one problem . . ."

The torchlight fell on a picture of the ancient tribal team looking glum, holding their heads in shame.

"No matter how hard you tried . . ." Nooth smiled nastily, ". . . you just always ended up losing."

Dug looked at the paintings in dismay. One after another showed his ancestors conceding goal after goal, losing match after match.

"In fact, in the end," smirked Nooth, "you just gave up altogether! It was all too painful for you!"

The final painting showed a despairing player booting the rock ball far away, across a sea, to another land.

"You see," said Nooth, thoroughly enjoying himself, "it turns out your tribe was totally trash at soccer!"

"No!" gasped Dug. He stared at the cave walls in horror. "No! It can't be true."

The Tribe's hopes were built on the belief that they were descended from soccer heroes. Not losers.

Dug struggled to hold onto his faith in his friends. "Well, I still believe we can win!" he told Nooth defiantly, trying to sound like he meant it.

Nooth sneered at him. "Do you really, caveman? Because if you're wrong, there won't be any Tribe. These paintings will be all that's left of you."

Dug, looking miserable, didn't reply.

The torchlight flickered across Nooth's gloating face. He put an arm around Dug's shoulders, as if to reassure him. "But I'm willing to offer you a deal," he said slyly. "A way out."

Given what he now knew, Dug couldn't help being tempted. He listened, with a sinking heart, as Nooth spelled out his "deal."

Meanwhile, Hognob was proving once again just why he was early man's best friend. When Dug didn't return to the campfire party, Hognob had

gone looking for him. The clever hog had sniffed out Dug's scent. Sneaking past Bronze guards, he followed the trail to Bobnar's cave, and down into the mine. It led him, at last, to the painted cavern, and his missing friend.

Dug was alone in the gloom. Nooth had left him to think over his offer. Brooding on his grim options, Dug had become lost in dark thoughts. Visions of the Tribe slaving down in the mine tormented him.

"I'm so sorry, Chief!" Dug told the ghostly apparition of Bobnar that shimmered before him. "I didn't mean for this to happen!"

As he tried to grab his old friend by the shoulders, his nightmare dissolved . . .

. . . and he found himself clinging instead to Hognob, whose urgent nuzzling had brought Dug back to reality.

"Hognob!" cried Dug. He had never been happier to see his faithful pal. "My dear old hoggy friend!" He gave Hognob a big hug. But as they separated, Dug's smile quickly faded.

"Listen," he told Hognob gravely. "I need you to go back."

Hognob looked dismayed. He whined in protest, shaking his snout.

"Yes!" said Dug sadly. "Your place is with the others now. Forgive me, Hognob, but I've got a deal to make . . ."

Dug had made up his mind. The fateful soccer match had been his idea. If the Tribe lost, and his friends were forced to live out their lives down in Nooth's mine, it would be his fault. He couldn't let that happen.

"I've got to save the Tribe!" he told Hognob, with a resolute look.

As Dug turned and hurried away, his best friend's howls echoed around the great gloomy cavern behind him.

CHAPTER ELEVEN

DUG'S CHOICE

In the Bronze City, the atmosphere was electric. The day of the big match had arrived at last, and the place was buzzing.

Excited citizens, making their way to the match, thronged the street that led to the great central stadium. The cries of the officials at its entrance rang out over the general hubbub.

"One hundred schnookels! One hundred schnookels!"

"Voluntary contribution! Everyone has to pay!"

Lord Nooth had not hesitated in doubling the ticket price. He was confident his people would pay handsomely to watch this unique match, and he was right. There was a good deal of grumbling among the fans lining up, but none were prepared to miss their famous home team taking on an unknown Stone Age squad. They all dug deep to find the necessary bronze.

Nooth was already reveling in the riches the match was bringing in. He was up in his private box with his assistant, Dino, drooling over an overflowing coin chest.

"Ah, it's all going to plan, Dino!" he sighed happily, letting a handful of coins run through his fingers.

Nooth was so entranced by his beloved bronze that he failed to notice the *Taran-Tara!* of a fanfare from the street outside the stadium.

He took a schnookel from the chest and pressed it to his lips. "*Mmwa!* I love you, little bronze coin!" he slobbered. Eyes shining, he caressed several more coins, kissing each in turn. "And you . . . *Mmwa!* And you!"

His smile faded at the sound of a familiar voice nearby.

"What a mammoth journey!" it declared regally. "Where's Nooth?"

Lord Nooth rolled his eyes in irritation. "Not

that stupid old bird again?" he groaned. Queen Oofeefa had evidently sent her annoying bird with another nagging message. Nooth did not intend to listen to it. "Tell Chef to boil it up in a cassoulet!" he ordered Dino, continuing to admire his coins.

There was no reply. Nooth glanced around to check Dino had understood . . .

. . . and got a rather nasty shock.

It was not Queen Oofeefa's talking bird he had heard. It was the queen herself. She was glaring at Nooth from her magnificent royal carriage. It had pulled up inside the stadium, right in front of his box.

"Stupid old bird?" echoed the Bronze monarch. There was an icy look in her narrowed eyes. "Cassoulet?"

"Y-Your Majesty!" spluttered Nooth, doing his best to hide his alarm with a forced smile. He hastily hid the coin-chest, too, shoving it out of the queen's sight. "This is an unexpected . . ."

A red-carpeted drawbridge swung down from the royal carriage and landed on Nooth's foot.

". . . pleasure," he finished, through gritted teeth.

Queen Oofeefa swept grandly across the drawbridge, crushing Nooth's toes beneath it.

"I thought I'd come to this caveman match myself," said the queen. She pinched Nooth's nose between her finger and thumb. "To have a little nose around," she told him, smiling sweetly.

Two men came trotting across the drawbridge after the queen, squashing Nooth's foot some more. They were enclosed in a mobile wooden booth equipped with the latest voice-boosting gadgetry. These were Queen Oofeefa's royal commentators, Bryan-with-a-y and Brian-with-an-i.

"And you have to say, Brian," observed the former as they passed the grimacing Nooth, "Real Bronzio's manager is really on the back foot!"

"Terrible start for the lad, Bryan," agreed Brian-with-an-i. "I put it down to pre-match nerves."

Queen Oofeefa made herself comfortable in Nooth's usual place of honor. All around the great soccer stadium, people were taking their seats. The stands were packed. The vast crowd gave a mighty roar as a grand fanfare heralded the start of the main event.

"Right . . . well . . ." said Nooth, "Let's start the fun, shall we?" His main concern now was to distract the queen from spotting his hastily hidden schnookels.

He moved to the front of the balcony to begin the pre-match ceremony.

"Bring out the Stone Age captain!" he commanded.

Dug stood waiting in the mouth of the players' tunnel. A shove from his burly Bronze guards sent him stumbling into the arena. He walked miserably out onto the field, to his doom.

"WHO CHALLENGES THE CHAMPIONS?" demanded Nooth pompously.

Dug took a deep breath. He stepped forward to pick up the ceremonial spear of the Challenger. This was the moment of truth. If he went through with the deal he had reluctantly agreed to with Nooth, there could be no turning back. It would mean a life of slavery for him, but it would save the rest of the Tribe from sharing his fate. Nooth had promised to leave them in peace, as long as Dug played his part. What choice did he have?

He raised the Challenger's spear high . . .

. . . then let the hand holding it drop limply to his side.

"NOT ME!" he yelled.

There were murmurs of surprise all around the stadium.

"I FORFEIT THE MATCH AND VOLUNTEER MYSELF FOR THE MINES!" declared Dug, as Nooth had instructed.

Up in his box, Lord Nooth made an exaggerated show of shock and astonishment.

The buzz of the crowd quickly turned into a loud chorus of boos and jeers. This was not what the fans had paid good bronze to see.

Queen Oofeefa shared her people's angry frustration. She had come a long way for this match. She was not used to being disappointed. She glared frostily at Nooth.

"Have the cavemen caved?" she said, scowling.

"So it seems. How very disappointing!" said Nooth, doing his best to look like he meant it. He was not in the least bit disappointed. This was exactly how he had planned for things to go. The match was off, but the schnookels were in. He didn't care about the match. It was the money that mattered.

"Everyone go home! There's no match!" he shouted from the balcony, then lowered his voice to speak slyly to the nearest of his guards. "Tell the staff—no refunds."

As Dug listened to the crowd's angry jeering, and saw Nooth smirking triumphantly down at him, he had never felt more alone. The knowledge that he would never see the Tribe again, not even his best pal Hognob, was hard to bear. He hung his head in misery.

A moment later, however, a loud yell of surprise made him look up. The cry had come from Nooth's assistant, Dino. He was staring at the sky, pointing in amazement. Dug followed Dino's wide-eyed gaze.

What he saw made his own jaw drop, his heart soar, and the ceremonial spear slip from his hand.

CHAPTER TWELVE

GAME ON!

"**F**owl!" yelled Dino, jabbing a finger at the sky. He blew a blast—*phweeeeeep!*—on his referee's whistle to get everyone's attention. "FOWL!"

Lord Nooth scowled at his overexcited assistant. "What do you mean, 'foul?'" he snapped. "No one's even playing, you silly slaphead!"

"No . . . FOWL!" repeated Dino, pointing skyward with even more urgency.

As his puzzled boss lifted his gaze, the rest of the crowd looked up, too.

A giant fowl, a monster-sized duck, was circling in the clear sky above. Several figures were perched on its feathered back. Nine of them were dressed in red-and-white soccer uniforms. The tenth, who appeared to be piloting the huge bird, was an elderly fellow in a green goalkeeper's shirt.

"Well, Bryan," announced Brian-with-an-i over the commentary system. "It looks like the Stone Age team has just flown in."

"Yes, Brian," agreed Bryan-with-a-y. "They're definitely looking good in the air!"

The giant duck began its landing approach. As it came swooping down toward the arena, Nooth watched, dumbstruck.

Queen Oofeefa fixed him with a withering look. She was running out of patience. Her Royal Highness did not like surprises.

"So . . ." she said frostily, "It seems there is a match after all!" She raised a royal eyebrow.

"Oh, happy day," replied Nooth, with another forced smile. Then he let out a shriek of horror as—*Splat!* The low-flying duck deposited a large quantity of sticky white poop right on his bald head.

Down on the field, Dug watched in open-mouthed amazement as the duck settled on the grass. His friends hastily dismounted and came striding over to join him. Hognob's enthusiastic greeting nearly bowled him over.

"Planning on starting without us, Dug?" asked Bobnar, grinning at Dug's stunned expression.

Dug's first reaction to his friends' surprise arrival was pure delight. As his mind turned, however, his spirits sank once more. The Tribe thought they were ready to face Real Bronzio. They hadn't seen the paintings Nooth had shown him. They didn't know the awful truth.

"Chief, we can't play this game!" Dug told Bobnar desperately. If they did, the entire Tribe would surely end up down in Nooth's horrible mine.

"What?" said Bobnar, still smiling. "Because of a few old cave paintings?"

For a second time, Dug looked gobsmacked.

"So . . . you know about those terrible pictures?" he said.

The Tribe had Hognob to thank for that. The moment Dug had left the Valley mine to face his lonely fate, Hognob had hurried back to the Badlands camp to find Bobnar. He had made the baffled old chief accompany him back to the painted cavern. Seeing the pictures there, Bobnar had easily guessed what Dug's reaction to them had been. The chief had rallied the Tribe as quickly as possible to go to their friend's aid. Thanks to their daring duck-flight, they had made it to Bronze City in time to face their mighty opponents, together.

"You're right, Dug," said Bobnar. "Those pictures are terrible. I can draw better than that!" He laid a reassuring hand on Dug's shoulder. "But that's all they are. Pictures." He gestured to the rest of the Tribe. "It's this group that counts," he said earnestly. "And you've given them hope, Dug."

There was a steely look on Bobnar's white-whiskered face as he turned to address the others.

"Let's go and paint our own story!" he cried. "For the Valley!"

The Tribe responded with an enthusiastic roar of team spirit . . .

. . . which died out rather abruptly as the mighty giants of Real Bronzio fell into line opposite them. The likes of Jurgund, the team captain, and his rugged teammates were not intimidated by Stone Age bravado. They leered menacingly at the Tribe.

"Actually," muttered Bobnar, having second thoughts, "they do look pretty tough."

Up in his box, Nooth had managed to wipe most of the duck poop from his head. He was seething. He no longer cared that his plan to have

Dug forfeit the match had backfired. All he wanted now was to see the cavemen humiliated. And why settle for one slave for his mine when he could have a whole tribe? He had, after all, always intended to go back on his deal.

Nooth reached for a nearby lever and gave it a yank. Out on the field, a soccer ball rose through the centre spot trapdoor.

"Very well, caveman!" Nooth snarled down at Dug. "It's your funeral!"

With a nod, he signaled to Dino to get the match underway.

CHAPTER THIRTEEN

BRILLIANT BRONZIO

Dug stood beside the center spot, with the ball at his feet and his heart in his mouth. His anxious teammates were firing questions at him.

"What's the plan, Dug?"

"Are we sticking to our positions?"

"What formation, Dug?"

"Errrrm . . . I . . . err . . ." stammered Dug, flustered.

Goona had told the Tribe they could win this match. They just had to believe they could. But right now, as he looked anxiously from one grim-faced Real Bronzio player to the next, Dug was finding that tough. Their opponents looked ready and eager for battle.

Jurgund, their captain, glared scornfully at Dug. "Let's get this done," he growled.

Dino blew a shrill blast on his referee's whistle. An official flipped the huge sand-timer mounted on the stadium's giant scoreboard. There was a swell of noise from the excited crowd.

Dug kicked off with a short pass to Gravelle, who looked as nervous as he was. Gravelle controlled the ball clumsily, and . . .

"Huh?"

. . . had it stolen from her, in a flash, by Lightning Hammer. The Bronzio midfielder had moved with breathtaking speed to make the tackle.

Hammer set off upfield, toward the Tribe's goal. Dug sprinted after him, desperate to win the ball back. But Hammer was too fast. He played a perfectly weighted pass to Jurgund, who was making an attacking run, his golden hair streaming. Jurgund collected the pass expertly and used a smooth trick move to breeze past Thongo.

"Everyone get back!" yelled Dug.

Goona sprinted up beside him. "Don't we need

someone up front?" she asked. "For the counter attack?"

"It's too risky!" Dug insisted.

The scrambling Stone Age players did their best to intercept Jurgund's weaving run, and failed. Jurgund dribbled into the penalty box, took the ball effortlessly past the last man, Asbo, and fired in a superb shot.

Bobnar made a brave attempt at a save, but the ball curled past his outstretched fingertips, into the back of the net.

The crowd went wild.

Their triumphant roar drowned out the *phweeeep!* of Dino's whistle. Goalscorer Jurgund soaked up the adoration of the fans as his celebrating teammates came running to smother him with hugs and kisses.

One of the scoring officials cranked a handle to make the scoreboard read 1 to 0. Hardly any sand had trickled through the match timer, and Real Bronzio was already a goal up.

"Ohhhh . . . my word, Bryan!" declared Brian-with-an-i. "Real Bronzio really caught their opponents napping!"

The Tribe looked at one another, awestruck.

The speed and ease with which their opponents had opened the scoring had left them shaken.

It was only a matter of minutes before Real Bronzio scored again.

And again.

"Goal number three!" announced Brian-with-an-i, chirpily. "Let's see the replay . . ."

Down in the arena, a small-scale replica of the field, mounted on a cart, was swiftly trundled out into the center circle. It was manned by the Action Replayers—a troupe of puppeteers. Using puppet versions of the players, they set about staging a slow-motion reenactment of the goal.

By now, the home fans were in a jubilant mood. The cavemen were getting well and truly thumped. Up in his private box, Nooth looked on in smug delight, wondering why he had ever been in the least bit worried about the match. Queen Oofeefa was having a grand old time, too, tooting away enthusiastically on a vuvuzela.

The desperate Tribe looked to their captain.

"Help us!" they pleaded.

But Dug was lost in his own panic and despair at how badly things were going. He could find no words of instruction or inspiration.

It was the fourth goal that seemed to seal the Tribe's fate.

It came in the closing seconds of the first half. This time the glory went to Lightning Hammer. After a dazzling solo run, he let loose a fearsome shot. Bobnar somehow got his body behind it, only to be driven into the back of his net so hard that the entire goal collapsed on top of him, knocking him out cold.

Dino blew a single whistle blast to award the goal, then three more to signal it was half-time. As the scoreboard was updated to a humiliating 4 to 0, Dug and his downhearted teammates hurried to the aid of their injured chief.

Up in Nooth's box, Bryan-with-a-y summed up the first half.

"I'll tell you what, Brian, the Stone Age team is in total disarray!"

No one was enjoying the Tribe's humiliation more than Lord Nooth. He was getting rather carried away.

"That's why you're going down!" he jeered, wagging the giant finger of his foam hand in time with his chant. "That's why you're going down . . . the mine!"

The mood of the Tribe, as they skulked off down the tunnel for the break, was very different to that in Nooth's box. They had to carry Bobnar to the changing room on a stretcher. He lay still, eyes closed, moaning weakly. Dug knelt anxiously over him. The others looked on with gloomy faces.

"This is all my fault . . ." muttered Dug miserably, as he mopped the old chief's brow with a sponge. He saw Bobnar's eyelids flicker open. "Chief?"

"Dug . . ." croaked Bobnar, with effort. His eyes were bleary, his voice weak. "Promise me, when this is all over . . . when we get back to the Valley, we'll go hunting . . . like the good old days . . ."

Dug had a lump in his throat and tears in his eyes as he replied.

"I promise, Chief. We'll go rabbit hunting."

Bobnar's eyes widened. He grasped Dug's arm, struggling to sit up.

"No, Dug! Not rabbit hunting! Mammoth hunting!" he insisted. "I was wrong to . . . we should be . . . mammoth hunting . . ."

He fell back, and lay still.

"Chief?" cried Dug, fearing the worst. "Chief!"

The others' faces filled with sadness.

A moment later, to their enormous relief, Bobnar began to snore.

"I think he's worn out," said Gravelle.

"Well," said Treebor, "he *is* nearly thirty-two!"

Magma looked puzzled. "What did he mean?" she asked, frowning. "About mammoth hunting?"

Dug had no wish to discuss his ambitious idea. It seemed to him that his ideas only caused trouble. "He's a bit confused, that's all," he told Gravelle.

"No," snapped a voice behind him. "He's not!"

The Tribe turned. Goona was standing with her hands on her hips, and a feisty look on her face.

"He's not confused at all," she said. "He's spot on." She began to pace up and down, fixing her stern glare on each of her teammates in turn. "That's your problem. You're acting like rabbit-hunters out there!" Reaching Dug, she jabbed a finger at him. "Especially you!"

Dug felt a stab of shame.

"You've stopped believing," said Goona to Dug accusingly. "And if you don't believe, how do you expect them to?"

Dug knew, in his heart, that his Bronze Age friend was right.

"The only way to beat giants is to think big," insisted Goona. "Think like—"

"Like mammoth hunters . . ." murmured Dug. His sense of self-belief and purpose came flooding back. He stepped forward to stand beside Goona, and turned to face the others. Determination shone in his eyes once more.

"Goona's right," he told his friends. "This Tribe's done playing safe!"

Out in the arena, a fanfare marked the end of the interval.

It was time for the second half of the match.

Time to go hunt mammoths.

CHAPTER FOURTEEN

THE TRIBE, UNITED

Once again, the Bronze and Stone Age teams faced off in the seconds before kick-off. This time, Dug held Jurgund's fierce glare with his own steady, steely gaze. The Tribe, he was determined, were about to show Real Bronzio just what cavemen could do.

"Looks like a change in tactics for the cavemen," observed Brian-with-an-i. "They're pushing every-one forward."

The most important change Dug had made was in his own attitude. His anxiety and indecision were gone. He was once more his old, bold self—full of purpose, energy, and confidence.

"We can still do this!" Dug told his teammates with conviction. "We can bring down a mammoth!"

As he gave out instructions, making full use of Goona's advice, the rest of the Tribe quickly took on his determined mood.

At the sound of Dino's whistle, Real Bronzio kicked off . . .

. . . and the Tribe surged forward to press for the ball.

Jurgund dribbled expertly toward the timid Treebor. With a slick side-step, he went past him . . .

. . . and found, to his surprise, that he no longer had the ball. Treebor, for once, had stood his ground and tackled the Bronzio captain. He quickly hit a long pass into the path of Asbo, who was sprinting upfield along the wing.

Asbo wove past one player, then another, using the skills he had learned dodging Badlands geysers. He sent a looping cross into the Real Bronzio box.

The Bronzio goalkeeper, Hugelgraber, had seen no action whatsoever in the first half of the match, and wasn't expecting to be called upon in the second. As Grubup came charging onto the end of Asbo's cross, he caught the keeper napping.

"Goal! Yum! Me score!" cried Grubup happily,

booting the ball past the surprised Hugelgraber, into the back of the net.

The referee blew for a goal. The Tribe went wild.

Their cheering was the only sound in the arena. A stunned silence had fallen over the Bronze Age crowd.

Queen Oofeefa was not amused. She glared at Lord Nooth.

"Beginners' luck, Your Majesty," Nooth assured her nervously.

The scoreboard official was struggling to get the seized-up visitors' score number to move. By the time it had creaked to a 1, a scowling Jurgund was already striding back toward the center spot with the ball.

"Bad move, caveman!" he growled menacingly at Dug as the teams took up their positions for the restart. "Now you've made us mad!"

The whistle sounded.

Jurgund received the ball and immediately took a mighty long-range shot. As the ball sailed toward the Tribe's goal, Dug realized, to his horror, that there was no one there to stop it. With Bobnar out injured, the Tribe had no goalkeeper.

The ball was dropping toward the open goal . . .

. . . when a furry figure in full keeper's uniform leaped from nowhere to make a stunning last-gasp save.

"Hognob!" cried Dug, beaming. He rushed to embrace his four-legged pal. "Incredible save, my dear old hoggy friend! You're in the team!"

Dino hurriedly consulted his rulebook. Having satisfied himself that hogs were, in fact, allowed on the field, he waved to keep playing.

Hognob cleared the ball with a stylish scorpion kick. Dug urged the others upfield, into attack.

Goona smiled to herself as the Tribe pressed forward, dribbling and passing with confidence. This was more like it.

"Remember the training!" she called.

The nearest Real Bronzio player gave her a suspicious look. Goona had not thought to match her voice to her caveman disguise. She quickly tried again.

"Remember the training!" she repeated, in her gruffest, manliest growl.

And they did. Their Badlands sessions were really paying off. Eemak's fast footwork, perfected by hours of boulder-dodging, caught up the Bronzio defenders trying to close him down. He fired in a shot . . .

. . . and the ball rocketed past the diving Hugelgraber for a second time.

As another shocked silence fell over the Bronze Age fans, Eemak sprinted across to his whooping teammates for his goalscoring reward.

"Waiyaiyayupkissykissyhughug!"

Up in Nooth's box, Queen Oofeefa had a face like thunder. Scowling, she snapped her vuvuzela in half. Nooth swallowed nervously.

The Tribe were in full flow now. As play continued, they showed increasing flair and spirit, and the mood in the stadium slowly began to change. The unique playing style of the Stone Age visitors made them enormous fun to watch.

Magma took on the full back, scaring the life out of him. She chipped the ball into the box . . .

. . . and a brilliant diving header from Gravelle brought the scoreline to 4 to 3. As Gravelle celebrated her goal with some tribal dance moves, there was applause, not silence, from the stands.

The Tribe's plucky fight back was winning over the commentary team, too.

"Real Bronzio just don't know what's hit them,

Brian!" declared Bryan-with-a-y. "The Stone Age team is really coming together!"

"I'll say, Bryan! It's like early man, united!"

Even Queen Oofeefa was impressed. "I have to admit," she observed, leaning forward to see better, "the cavemen are rather entertaining!"

It was Goona's stunning equalizer, a few minutes later, that really brought the crowd to life.

"Oh, look at this!" cried Brian-with-an-i, as Goona went on a weaving solo run toward the Bronzio goal. "The Stone Age striker beats one . . . nutmegs another . . . this player's going all the way . . . GOALLLLLL!"

The stadium erupted into cheers and applause.

Down on the field, Goona was living out her dream.

"Yup. This is just how I imagined it," she told Dug as she beamed and waved at the clapping, whooping fans. "No. It's better!"

In her excitement, she tore off her caveman disguise.

Watching from his box, Nooth had been getting more livid with every goal the Tribe scored. Now he gave a cry of outrage. "Wait a minute! She's one of ours!" he shrieked. "And she shouldn't even be on the field!"

Queen Oofeefa, a champion of girl power, glared at him.

"Why not, exactly?" she asked, icily.

"Because she's a . . . she's a g . . ." Nooth faltered as he read the queen's expression. ". . . G-g-reat player," he finished feebly, forcing a smile. "Play on!"

As the match resumed, the miserable Nooth reached a decision. With the scores now level, desperate measures were called for. He quietly slipped from his seat and slunk out of the box, hoping the queen was too distracted to notice.

Queen Oofeefa did notice, however. Glancing around, she also noticed something else—a chest, partly hidden behind Nooth's vacated seat.

Down on the field, the two teams once again took up their positions for a restart after the goal. Dug glanced up to see how much sand was left in the top half of the match timer. Hardly any.

Just one more goal, thought Dug. *We can do this!*

Then his heart sank. A man in an ill-fitting referee uniform was hurrying across the field to oversee the restart, but it wasn't Dino.

It was Lord Nooth.

"Dino is having a rest," declared Nooth. "I'm the new ref."

He didn't mention the reason Dino was having a "rest." In order to take his place, Nooth had lured him into the tunnel moments earlier, and knocked him out with his own heavy rule book.

"You can't be ref!" protested Dug. "That's not fair!"

Nooth ignored him. He blew for Jurgund to take the kick-off.

Now that their devious boss was refereeing, the Real Bronzio players knew they could get away with murder. As Jurgund dribbled upfield, his teammates carried out a series of shocking off-the-ball fouls to prevent any Stone Age player from challenging him.

Nooth was deaf to the appeals of the outraged Tribe.

"I didn't see anything!" he said innocently. "Play on!"

Jurgund ran on, into the Tribe's penalty area, and, with no one near him, he immediately performed a dramatic dive, as though someone had tripped him. He writhed theatrically on the grass.

"Oh, my leg! My leg!" he wailed. "I'm dying!"

Goona scowled as Nooth blew for a foul. "We were nowhere near him!" she protested.

Nooth smiled slyly. "Let's check the replay . . ." he suggested.

The Action Replayers hurried out onto the field. A look from Nooth told them what was expected. Their puppet "replay" bore no resemblance to the truth. Instead, it clearly showed that several cavemen had brought Jurgund down by beating him with sticks.

"Oh! Terrible foul!" lied Nooth, shaking his head. "PENALTY!" he declared, pointing to the spot.

Dug's heart sank. With a single shameless piece of cheating, Nooth had turned the tide of the match.

The Tribe were now one kick away from defeat. One kick away from losing their home and their freedom.

CHAPTER FIFTEEN

CHAMPIONS!

Lord Nooth's obvious cheating did not go down well with either the crowd or Queen Oofeefa. There were loud boos from the fans, and a scowl on the queen's face. The Sacred Game was supposed to be played fairly.

But by fair means or foul, Real Bronzio was on the brink of victory. Dug's heart raced as Jurgund prepared to take the penalty. In the goalmouth, Hognob bravely did his best to distract the striker.

Jurgund took his run up and . . . *Thwack!* Hit a superb shot, low and hard. It rocketed toward the corner of the goal . . .

. . . only to be blocked by an outstretched trotter as the diving Hognob made a heroic save.

The deflected ball flew high into the air. As Dug's eyes followed it, he heard the voice of Bobnar echo in his mind. "Dug! Dug! Never stop believing!" it urged him.

Dug suddenly realized that the words weren't just in his mind. He glanced to the touchline from where Bobnar, much recovered, was yelling at him.

"WE'RE A MAMMOTH-HUNTING TRIBE, DUG!"

Dug looked back to the ball. It was beginning to drop. He knew what he had to do.

Just as in his first match in the Bronze stadium, time seemed suddenly to slow. Dug battled against Bronzio players to get to the falling ball first. He leaped high. Twisting his body in mid-air, he performed a dramatic, acrobatic overhead kick.

This time, his technique was perfect.

The ball rocketed off Dug's cleat, away from the Tribe's goal. Following a long, high arc, it flew the full length of the field . . .

. . . over the head of the dismayed Hugelgraber . . .

. . . and into the back of the Real Bronzio net!

There was a moment of stunned silence, then the crowd erupted. Queen Oofeefa leaped to her feet with the rest, applauding wildly.

"Amazing goal!" screamed Brian-with-an-i.

Down on the field, Dug was being mobbed by his overjoyed teammates. The giant duck, who had taken on the role of team mascot, waddled over to join the Tribe's celebration.

"The giant duck's on the field!" cried Bryan-with-a-y. "He thinks it's all over!"

"It is now!" declared Brian-with-an-i, as the final whistle sounded. Dino, coming to, had staggered onto the field in his undies and blown the whistle signaling the game was over.

The shattered Real Bronzio players collapsed on the grass, as dejected as the Tribe were triumphant. Dug saw Jurgund lying miserably nearby. He broke free from the huddle of his whooping friends and went over to the Bronzio captain. He held out his hand.

"Good game," said Dug, smiling.

Jurgund looked surprised. After a moment's hesitation, he took Dug's hand. Dug helped him up.

"Ya," said Jurgund. "Well played."

Asbo followed Dug's example. "Great game! Champion!" he beamed, hugging the surprised Lightning Hammer.

Thongo was swapping an overpoweringly smelly shirt with Gonad, when an angry cry made them all turn.

"Cheater!" yelled Dino, red-faced with outrage, as he ripped his referee's uniform from Lord Nooth's body.

Nooth, now in just his underwear, scowled back. "Baldie!" he screamed at Dino.

Their squabbling was silenced by the arrival on the field of Queen Oofeefa herself. Her royal attendants were carrying Nooth's brimming coin-chest. They set it down on the grass in front of him.

"Nooth!" demanded the queen, fixing him with an icy stare. "Have you been using the Sacred Game to line your own pockets?"

Nooth, growing pale, had no answer.

"Yes, Your Majesty!" said Goona, stepping up. "These cavemen have shown us what soccer should be about." She glared fiercely at Nooth. "But all he cares about is bronze!"

There were cheers and murmurs of agreement

from the listening crowd. Queen Oofeefa had a decisive look.

"Lord Nooth," she declared grandly, "you are hereby relieved of your command!" With a flourish, she produced a red card and held it high, glowering at Nooth. Then she turned her back on him in regal contempt.

"Oh! It's the red card for the Real Bronzio manager!" announced Brian-with-an-i.

"And he's off to the mines, Brian . . . no question!" confirmed his co-commentator.

Lord Nooth did not accept his dismissal honorably. Even as the commentators proclaimed his fate, he was slyly attempting to grab his precious schnookels and sneak away before anyone realized.

His escape came to a swift and undignified end. The giant duck, at Bobnar's bidding, went after him. It snatched Nooth up in its mighty beak and shook him so hard that his ill-gotten schnookels were scattered far and wide, showering the cheering crowd.

With Nooth dealt with, Queen Oofeefa turned her royal attention to Dug.

"Well," she said, in a friendlier tone. "It seems you cavemen aren't so primitive after all."

Dug grinned. "We've got more in common than you'd think," he replied politely.

"Like a love for the Beautiful Game!" agreed the queen. "Speaking of which, I believe this is yours."

With a smile, she presented Dug with a magnificent trophy. It was made from an ancient, soccer ball-shaped rock. As Dug gazed at it in wonder, Goona, Hognob, Bobnar, and the rest of the Tribe crowded around to marvel at it.

Beaming, Dug raised the trophy high over his head. A deafening roar filled the Bronze City stadium. It was the sort of noise that soccer fans make for only one kind of team . . .

. . . CHAMPIONS!

EPILOGUE

OVERTIME

The sun shines brightly on a beautiful forested valley. In a clearing in the trees stands a smart, newly built clubhouse, beside a freshly painted soccer field.

Standing stones are dotted around the clearing. Some are covered with ancient, faded paintings. One has been painted recently. It shows a happy, celebrating group, lifting a trophy above their heads.

Several fur-clad figures are relaxing in the morning sunshine. Their smiling faces look very much like those of the figures in the rock painting.

They are watching a puppet show acted out on a miniature soccer field.

"A historic day, Brian," one of the troupe of puppeteers has his puppet say, as another makes his blonde-haired player puppet run jerkily out onto the field. "The first time a girl has played for Real Bronzio!"

"And what a bright future she has, Bryan!" adds a second puppet commentator.

There is a cave entrance at one side of the clearing. An elderly, white-haired man steps out from the cave, into the sunlight. He calls to the others to gather around. A little reluctantly, they agree to watch the rest of the replay of their friend's historic debut later, when she can enjoy it with them.

They gather in a circle.

As the group bow their heads, their chief leads them in their daily blessing. They give thanks for their precious home, so nearly lost. They vow to learn from past mistakes; to grow as a tribe; to look outwards, not inwards; and to be happy to share their bountiful home with others.

And then, together, they set out on a hunt . . . A mammoth hunt.